THE
Joining of the
Stone

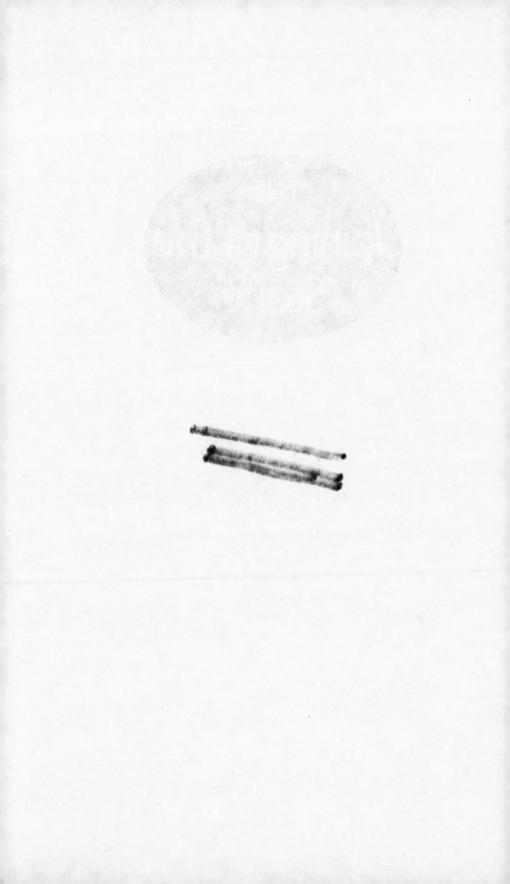

THE
Joining of the
Stone

by
Shirley Rousseau
Murphy

*Atheneum * New York*
1981

LIBRARY OF CONGRESS CATALOGING IN PUBLICATION DATA

Murphy, Shirley Rousseau.
The joining of the stone.

"An Argo book."
SUMMARY: Lobon, son of Ramad of the Wolves, helped
by the wolves and the Seers of Carriol,
continues his father's struggle to find the shards
of the runestone and unite them for the power of good.
Sequel to "Caves of Fire and Ice."
[1. Fantasy] I. Title.
PZ7.M956Jo   [Fic]   81–2351
ISBN 0–689–30822–1   AACR2

Published simultaneously in Canada by
McClelland & Stewart, Ltd.
Manufactured by
The Fairfield Graphics, Fairfield, Pennsylvania
Designed by M. M. Ahern
First Edition

Contents

Part One
Ramad's Heir
5

Part Two
Heritage of the Dark
69

Part Three
The Joining
119

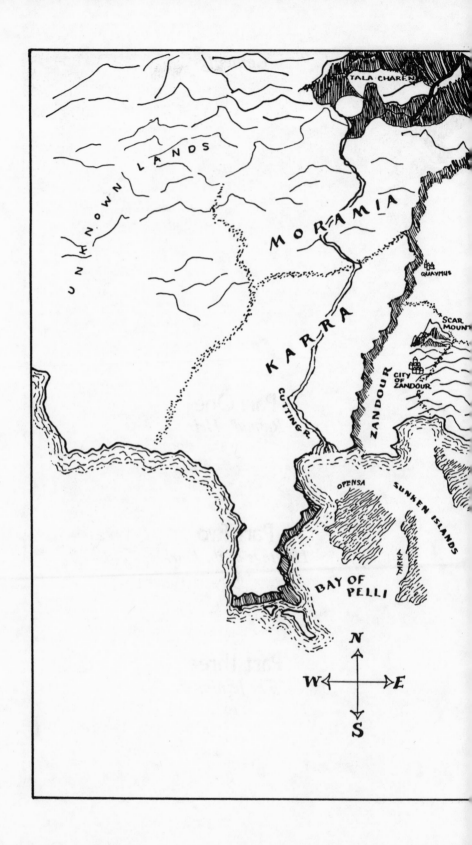

MAP of ERE

Early pages from the Journal of Skeelie of Carriol:

Why do I write these words? No one I know will ever see them. Everyone from my own time—except Ramad—was long dead when first I knew that I had moved through Time into an unknown future. I didn't think of loneliness then, I knew or cared for nothing but Ram. And I searched for him through Time that carried him and used him in ways I could not have imagined.

Was Time unlocked by Ram's need, for it to take him so readily? By Ram's love for Telien? Perhaps some day I can write of those cataclysmic flingings through Time, but now I can only mourn Ram.

Ramad is dead. Ramad of the wolves is dead. My love is dead, and I can only mourn him with the same pain that, eight years gone in our lives, he mourned the death of Telien.

I have come away from the abyss of fire, having buried Ramad beside it. I have brought our son here to the city of cones. I need to be near people for a little while, if only these simple folk. I write these words in a small cone house they have given me. Torc and Rhymannie doze by my feet before the fire as complacent as dogs, for these folk have accepted the wolves just as they accepted Lobon and me, gently and unquestioning. Fawdref is not with us—Fawdref master of his pack, Fawdref who loved Ram so. He is buried beside Ram, in a grave that was once our home. Rhymannie mourns him just as I mourn Ram. Their big cubs and the rest of the pack roam the hills at this moment, hunting our dinner meat. I cannot take my mind from the rocky valley where Ramad lies and where we lived in happiness for eight years that seem no longer now than a day. I cannot take my mind from the fiery pit where Ram died, nor tear my soul from him.

The demon Dracvadrig is gone from the pit, or I would have sought him there and done my best to kill him. He carries with him the one shard of the runestone that Ramad fought to win, and I carry the four that Ram put in my keeping.

Would I have gone to kill Dracvadrig that day had he remained? Truly, I don't know. I know now only that all my strength must be for our son, that I must give Lobon all that Ram would have given him of training, of skill and of strength. He has the stubbornness, he has shown that plainly enough. He is only six, but as stubborn and fierce already as any young wolf cub could be. Can I temper and direct that willfulness? But I must. He is Ramad's heir—heir to Ram's commitment, heir to the joining of the runestone. Heir to the joining of those nine shards, if ever they can be brought together.

Ram died too soon. He died with the stone still asunder.

These four shards that I hold are Lobon's legacy. If Ram's life meant anything, then these stones must be used one day to turn the fate of Ere away from darkness. One shard more lies drowned in the sea. One lies hidden in darkness, lost by Telien I know not where. And there are two shards to which I have no clue. Dracvadrig carries his shard in a metal casket around his neck, the chain dangling past his waist when he is a man, and pulling tight across his scaly throat when he takes the dragon form. Nine shards of jade. Nine shards of power that must somehow be joined again, and our son heir to the skills and to the nature of that joining.

Meanwhile, dark eats upon the land, flaunting the runestone's broken, weakened powers. And Lobon frightens me; his violent nature, so filled with cold fury at Ram's death, frightens me. If such anger does not abate, his powers as a Seer cannot grow. I must learn to temper that anger; I must learn to strengthen the man in him. I must learn to do for Lobon what Ramad would have known to do. When I take up sword again, to teach him its skills, I must train his spirit as well. And when I teach him the Seeing powers, I must teach him patience and wisdom—just as skillfully as Gredillon the white-haired once taught the child Ramad, in a time long dead.

Where we will go from this place, I have no idea. It is enough

*just now to rest and try to ease the wound of Ram's death. I am
filled with tears, and I cannot weep. I know deep within that I will
survive the pain, but my spirit does not believe that. I know I must
mend, for Lobon, but I have not the heart to mend.*

*If no eyes but mine see this journal, still it helps to set forth my
thoughts; it eases something in me. The time of Lobon's manhood will
come too soon, and there is a cold fear in me of that time that I
cannot put aside.*

Part One

Ramad's Heir

Chapter
One

LOBON STOOD TALL above the boulder-strewn valley, his sword sheathed, his leather cape thrown back, looking down coldly upon the waste of lifeless stone. The valley, just as he remembered it from childhood, looked as if a giant hand had ripped and shattered the stone, splitting it into grotesque and tumbled shapes across the dry scar of sand; and the whole valley itself was dwarfed by the shouldering mountains far to his right and the sheer black cliff that towered close on his left. Above that cliff, he could see the icy white apron of the glacier Eken-dep thrust against the dropping sun.

Behind him in the south, beyond the wild mountains and beyond a line of smoking volcanoes, lay the civilized nations of Ere. He had never seen them except in Seer's visions, sharp as reality itself. This valley was his home, where he was born and bred, though it was twelve years since he had looked upon it. Its fierce cruelty had not softened during those years since he was six. He saw it with the same distaste he had known then, and with the same hatred. The same fury at his father's death, for that fury had never abated.

Ahead, the valley ended abruptly at the edge of a gaping abyss, a chasm so immense that a man entering it would feel as small as a dew-ant. Fire ran at the bottom of the abyss in blood red rivers bursting forth from fractured stone. The air down there was smoke-dulled and tinted sullen red. You could travel down there if you knew well the way. Or the pit could take your life. The width of the fissure was so great that the far jagged edge was lost in smoky mist. The black cliff that blocked the western end of the abyss pushed down into it like an obsidian blade, cutting off the land beyond. He turned his gaze away from that cliff to search among the boulders ahead for his companions. When he spoke at last, his voice seemed no more than a whisper against the awful silence. "Crieba? Feldyn?"

The dog wolves moved into the open and paused, then looked back at him, black Feldyn like a shadow against the dark shadows cast by the falling sun, Crieba's silver coat caught in a last streak of light. The sun would soon be gone behind the glacier.

"Shorren?"

The white bitch wolf appeared from behind a boulder and smiled up at him, her eyes golden jewels.

"Can you find a place in this abysmal pile of stone where I can lay my head? Is there game?"

Feldyn spoke silently. *We scent rock hare, Lobon. A deer passed through some hours back, but is gone. You will eat rock hare again.* He and Crieba leaped ahead to find shelter, losing themselves quickly among jagged boulders. Shorren waited for Lobon and pushed her nose against him, her warm white muzzle nudging his arm. She was increasingly uncomfortable at the fury that filled him, tried with female stubbornness to gentle him. She could not endure his anger without pain to herself and would never cease to try to soothe him.

Man and wolf worked their way down between boulders, across the jagged valley toward the lip of the abyss. Soon they stood at the rim, bathed in the hot breath of the abyss, and in the feel of evil that rose from it. Lobon knew no words to describe his contempt for the master of that pit.

Here on the edge of the pit he had stood as a child of six, watching Ramad die, and now once more his mind and heart filled with the scene, come sharp to Seer's senses. Shorren's golden eyes censured him for his self-inflicted pain, but she remained silent in her mind and let him be. Feldyn joined them, tasted the heat from the pit, then looked eastward, raising his black muzzle. He keened suddenly with eerie voice, challenging the master of Urdd. Lobon's silent challenge joined him, his black eyes searching the pit, his mottled red hair flaming in the last light like a burning blaze.

When Lobon spoke again, his voice was like scuffed silk against the valley's silence. "He will die. Dracvadrig will die at my hand."

The bitch wolf snarled softly. Lobon ignored her censure. He stared down at her and willed her to listen. "I will kill him, Shorren! And I will sink this pit of fire back into the center of Ere from which it gapes, and that will be Dracvadrig's grave."

Shorren's thought came softly, but as steady as stone. *You are too arrogant, young whelp. You are too filled with the lust for revenge. That lust can blind you.* The dog wolves echoed her, Crieba slipping silently to Lobon's side; but Lobon turned from all three and closed his mind to their words. He pulled from his tunic a deerskin pouch, dark with age and brittle, and spilled out into his palm two long green shards of jade and five small amber stones. The smaller stones had, generations before, been cut from a similar shard.

The fourth shard was hidden inside the belly of the bronze bitch wolf that he took from his tunic, a rearing wolf with a bell suspended in her mouth. He lifted the bell, and it toned lightly, making the three wolves moan with its magic and stare up at him with rising light in their eyes.

Four shards of the runestone, Lobon held. The fifth, there below him in the pit, he meant to take from Dracvadrig very soon.

He followed Shorren and the two dog wolves to a rude tumble of boulders under which they might shelter from the creatures of the night sky: from the black flying lizards big as horses, and from the little blood-drinking night-stingers that hovered near the heat of the abyss. Twenty paces to his left stood the heaped stone that was the grave of Ramad. Once it had been Ramad's home, boulders with slabs of stone placed to roof a shelter. It would be dark inside now, sealed, attending the silence of death. Ramad's bones lay there, and Fawdref's bones. Lobon shivered, wished Ramad would step out of Time to him, move through Time as he had done before, across six generations. He did not understand Time and its limits. Ramad was dead here, in this time. A sickness and revulsion rose in him; he kept his distance from the grave and did not understand his own feelings.

He dropped his blanket and pack inside the smaller, rougher shelter, then turned back to the abyss and stood staring down, wanting to go down at once and pursue Dracvadrig and kill him, but knowing he must learn the abyss through visions first, learn Dracvadrig's nature better. Yet impatience ate at him and made him edgy. He began to pace. Shorren paced close to him, nuzzling him frequently as a mother would pat an unruly child.

They had been following Dracvadrig for twenty days, sensing the runestone Dracvadrig carried, Lobon drawn by the pull of the stone until he was nearly mad with it. They had climbed the face of Eken-dep following the master of Urdd, had stood halfway up the glacier only to see Dracvadrig transform himself from man to fire ogre and move on over the ice unfeeling of the cold, then at last transform himself into the dragon of fire he was famous for and leap from the glacier on giant wings laughing the laugh of a man. They had watched the creature fly down then into the abyss of fire; and there in the abyss Dracvadrig waited now, and Lobon would kill him there.

He had scant knowledge of Dracvadrig's nature. He knew only that the firemaster's skill at shape-changing was rare, and that the firemaster's cruelty was absolute. Was the creature a man, or a demon? Had Dracvadrig been born of living creatures? Or born of the elements of the abyss itself, born of fire and of sulfurous stone? Or born perhaps as twisted offspring from the seed of the mindless fire ogres?

Lobon cared little what the creature was, he knew only that Dracvadrig must die. If Skeelie were here, she would say, *You had better learn quickly Dracvadrig's nature, learn quickly what you face.* He thought of his mother and scowled, could see too plainly her thin, fine-boned face, the dark knot of hair falling over one shoulder. He felt the sense of her strength, in spite of his anger at her. They had parted in fury, not speaking; and later when he was away from her, he had not been able to bring himself to reach out in vision to mend that rift. Nor would he mend it now.

Yet it was Skeelie, thin and strong and torn apart inside, who had stood beside him here twelve years ago and seen Ramad die. Her suffering was as much a part of him as was his own.

Even so, he could not reach out. Her words when he left her had struck him like firebrands. "You are too driven by fury! It is madness to try alone! You need other Seers, there are those who would help you. You have only to reach out to them. Your pride is too great, your anger too sharp; you warp your judgement by such wrath. No *matter* that Canoldir feels he must let you go, you court failure, Lobon, to go alone in such violence of mind!" They had stood staring at one another locked in the burning torment born of love and of pain. Then he had turned and left her, left the home of Canoldir, left the ice mountains, and gone out of that land of Timelessness into a land where Time ran forward as men know it, the three wolves leaping down over ice cliffs leaving the rest of the pack to join him. And, once again in common time, he had begun to search out Dracvadrig by the sense of the runestone he carried, feeling the stone pull at him and not asking himself why it did.

After Dracvadrig flew away from the ice mountain, it had taken Lobon and the wolves three days to make their way back down the glacier and another day to reach the valley, across land so desolate it might never have known water or growing seed. Now at the brink of the abyss, Lobon began to feel clearly the desire with which Dracvadrig coveted his own four stones. He knew the firemaster would kill for them, and the knowledge infuriated him. "You are as good as dead!" Lobon said softly. "You are as dead as if the blood were already draining from your body."

But a voice rose thundering from the abyss, the shock of it like a sword slash. *"You are insolent, son of Ramad! You are untried and ignorant and weak!"* Cold sweat touched Lobon. *"What makes you dream, son of a bastard, that you can take my life!"*

Slowly Lobon stepped down to a lower, jutting lip along the precipice. Shorren moved with him and tried to press him back. Far below, a flaming river ran. Smoke drifted across broken rock. Shapes were lost in heat-warped air. There was no movement except drifting smoke. He tried to sense the direction of the voice, but Dracvadrig's laughter echoed, directionless. *"Do you imagine, child of a bastard, that you can see me when I do not choose to show myself? Do you imagine that you can kill me?"*

"I will snuff your life, master of Urdd," Lobon shouted, "as surely as a wolf can snuff a rock hare! And I will own the runestone to which you have no claim!"

"Ah, and you are heir to its joining!" Dracvadrig mocked, his laughter cold. *"Think you to join that stone, bastard's child? You? When the powers of seven generations have prevented that joining? The dark powers will prevent it, bastard's whelp, perhaps until Time ceases. The stone will never be joined until the dark itself chooses to join it for its own use!"*

"What care I for *any* such joining! I care only for the pleasure of seeing you die!"

"You are a fool, son of Ramad. And I take pleasure in that!" The firemaster's voice echoed harshly, then the abyss was silent. The weight of the towering black cliff seemed to bear down like lead toward Lobon. Silence spanned to eternity, and the firemaster did not speak again.

Only when Lobon moved back from the rim at last did Shorren ease her weight against him. He took the scruff of her neck in his hands, and she turned and locked her teeth on his arm, gentle as the fluttering of moths.

Once the wolves had gone to hunt, Lobon gathered greasebrush and animal droppings and built a small fire in the lee of the rock shelter they had found, then sat warming himself, looking across the abyss toward the deepening sky and the line of mountains beyond, where no man he knew of had ever ventured: not Ramad, not even the man who lived outside of Time who was his mother's lover. When the sun dropped behind the white face of Eken-dep, the rock-strewn valley changed from a place of sharp humping shadows to one of flat subdued light. The tumbled boulders seemed to recede and to shrink in size.

The evening turned chill. The emptiness of the land was overpowering. He leaned close to the fire, stricken with the idea suddenly that he might be the last man alive in all of Ere, alone at the edge of unknown spaces, unknown realities. Did death seep out of the abyss to give him such thoughts? He tried to put his unease aside, but the sense of Dracvadrig pushed around him to chill his mind until he felt heavy and inept.

Then at last he felt Dracvadrig drawing away from him, as if the firemaster was distracted or had turned his attention toward another. It seemed to him the firemaster was reaching out in another direction, touching a consciousness far distant. Lobon's mind quickened with interest, and he reached out toward that same vision, tried to immerse himself in the image that Dracvadrig's mind seemed to conjure so sharply, and in the rush of voices that accompanied it, disjointed and confused. All shifted senselessly, though Dracvadrig was mingling with the scenes comfortably enough, as if he had done this before. Where? Where were these Seers he conjured? Surely these were Seers, whose minds Dracvadrig touched so deftly. How could they remain unaware of the firemaster? The creature had blocking skills, powerful skills. He felt Dracvadrig begin to beguile one mind in particular, and to turn and shape its thoughts as if he were shaping clay. A girl. Young. Lobon could see her face, fine-boned, thin; dark hair falling across her shoulders loose and tangled as if from sleep. And her eyes were startling, huge and lavender like the wings of the mabin bird. Her skin was lightly tanned, but a streak of white shone where her hair parted behind one ear. Her cheeks were ruddy, the whole essence of her as brilliant in coloring as was the mabin bird. She was unaware of Lobon's scrutiny, and seemed aware of Dracvadrig only vaguely; though she was disturbed by him and by the darkness he drew around her, for she shuddered as if from a brutal touch. Yet there was an emptiness within her, too, something soft and malleable that made Dracvadrig easily welcome in spite of her revulsion. Lobon sensed people around her, the activity of a town. He could hear the sea crashing close by. He tried to touch the lower, dreaming levels of the girl's mind, tried to seek as Dracvadrig sought; but he could not touch her. Why did the dragon seek her out? What did she have that Dracvadrig wanted? Then suddenly the vision vanished, the sense of Dracvadrig faded. Lobon was alone, shivering in the cold darkness.

The fire had burned to embers. The wolves were pushing at him, returned from the hunt. Four rock hare lay at his feet. He looked at them muzzily, then knelt to build up the fire so he could see to skin out his supper.

Late in the night, long after he had gone to sleep, something awakened him so violently he jerked upright, scraping his arm against a boulder. He swore with the pain, was wide awake and sitting up staring into a path of moonlight that held two images: dry sand and stone outside the den; and the vision-image of a pale stone room. The girl was lying asleep on a narrow cot, and through the room's window, Ere's twin moons hung thin as crystal above the sea.

He could sense Dracvadrig touching the girl's mind with fingers like flame. He felt her confusion as she woke, watched her rise from her bed and cross the room to stare out at the moonlit sea. He felt her mindless compulsion, watched her turn at last and began to dress, then pull on a dark cloak, all the time trying to free herself from Dracvadrig's possession, but yet needing terribly to obey him.

He watched her leave the room and climb a flight of twisting stone steps to a huge, cavernous grotto washed with moonlight. He could hear the sea far below. In the center of the room stood a round stone table, and above it hung a stone on a long gold thread, a deep green stone, catching moonlight: a shard of the runestone of Eresu. This must be Carriol, then. This must be Carriol's runestone.

The girl shook her head, stared at the runestone, wanting it, coveting it. She tried to push Dracvadrig's dark compulsion away. Yet she needed to reach for the stone, needed desperately to touch it.

Still something held her back. She turned away at last, shaken, and made her way out and down the stairs.

Lobon sat puzzling. Why had Dracvadrig's power receded?

Surely the tower had been in Carriol, surely it was the tower at the ruins of Carriol, and this was Carriol's runestone, the only other stone in Ere now held and used by Seers. It had drawn Dracvadrig's covetous lust. But why had he let the girl go away without taking it? And why, when Lobon carried four shards, would the firemaster bother about Carriol's stone? Was he, then, so afraid of Lobon as to seek the power of a runestone elsewhere, to add to the power of the one he carried?

Was Dracvadrig *not* powerful enough to better him? Elated with the thought, Lobon burned to confront the firemaster.

He did not pause to think of the subtlety of the stones' powers, or that those powers could vary with forces that lay beyond them: with the strengths of those who wielded them, and with strengths far greater still, as yet only vaguely understood. He did not care to remember Skeelie's words or Canoldir's explaining the casual balances of those forces beyond the stones, beyond men, forces as mindless and natural as the erupting of Ere's heaving volcanoes. He thought only of his own power in the stones he carried, and of the foe he sought.

He set himself to studying with heated urgency the sense of the uncharted land deep in the abyss, the directions the fiery rivers took, the power of the land's upheavals. He studied the sense of Dracvadrig, turning at last from the girl and from Carriol's runestone, knew that the firemaster would return his mind-powers there. Then he felt Dracvadrig moving below in the abyss, slow and ponderous, waiting for him.

Chapter
Two

MEATHA WOKE to find herself standing in her moonlit room fully dressed, her cloak dragging from one shoulder. She was shaken and upset and did not know why, or where she had been. She was sure she had just come through the door, that she had been out in the chill halls of the tower. Her hands were cold, her cheeks numb with cold. She stood with her fist pressed to her lips, trying to make the image that clung in her mind come clear, something half-forgotten and upsetting; but it blew away like smoke. Where had she been? It was the middle of the night, the moons outside her window hung low above the sea, and she was fully dressed. Why? She had been walking, she was sure she had. She knelt to feel her boots and found them dry. Then an image of the shadowed citadel touched her mind, an image of the runestone, deep green, catching moonlight. Why had she been in the citadel?

Why? Why would she go there in the middle of the night, and then not remember? She shivered, stood staring absently at her rumpled cot.

She remembered going to bed, remembered snuffing the lamp. What could have waked her, made her dress and go from her room unknowing? Made her go to the citadel, then not remember going? A darkness clung within her mind as cold and repugnant as death.

Slowly, slowly she began to pull memory out of nothing,

until she knew at last that she had indeed stood pressing against the stone table staring at the suspended runestone, wanting to lift it down, her thoughts confused and frightened and at the same time wildly elated.

She had come away at last, she thought, against her own wishes. And why were her thoughts of the runestone afire with guilt? Surely she could go to look at the runestone if she wished; she herself had helped to bring it secretly to Carriol.

She left her room at last, too confused, too full of questions to sleep, and made her way down the inner stone stairway to a side door and out onto the moonlit ruins, her mind filled with thoughts that remained vague and shapeless and threatening. She walked slowly, head down, hardly seeing the broken stone rubble of the ruins, washed white with moonlight, stone that had once been towers, dwelling places. Behind her the great tower loomed, white and tall. She was on a high, narrow hump of land that separated Carriol from the sea. To her right and below lay the town. To her left, below jagged cliffs, the sea swung and pounded and flung moon-washed foam to break against the cliff. She stood staring down, caught in the sea's mindless rhythm, unable to escape her half-formed fears.

This was not the first time she had been somewhere she could not afterward remember, not the first time she had felt the brushing of cold shadow across her mind and not been able to capture the form of it. For days she had been edgy and uncertain, done badly at weapons practice, had been distracted in her work with Tra. Hoppa. And yesterday she had been so short-tempered and irritable with her young teaching charges that she had cut the class short. One could not teach Seers' skills with a mind as bristling as a sprika-shell. And she had been mean and bad-tempered with Zephy at a time when Zephy did not need that kind of distraction.

Now when she thought of Zephy's journey, even it made her uneasy; her fear rose suddenly and inexplicably as if chill hands had again touched her. She clenched her fist, frowning, trying to puzzle out what disturbed her.

This journey of Zephy and Thorn's *must* not be touched with darkness. This journey would be like none Carriol had sent out before, and if there was some terrible threat to it, she must see it. She tried, willing steadiness in her mind, willing herself to reach out.

She could see nothing. Only this unformed fear. Maybe it was nothing, then, maybe just her own unsettled state of mind.

Zephy and Thorn's journey would not be a fighting force sent out to help defend another nation against Kubal, nor even a trading party gathering intelligence. This journey would be a mission of friendship and dramatic showmanship designed to win the confidence of the new and puzzling cults that had risen so quickly across Ere; cults that no one, yet, understood, but that made all Carriol uneasy. She stood letting her mind wander, hardly aware of her own thoughts, until she noticed suddenly that the twin moons had dropped nearly to the horizon. She huddled into her cloak and watched the first touch of dawn begin to lighten the sky.

Soon a rosy light began to touch the cliff below her and to wash the fallen stones of the ruins where she stood. It reached down to the town below, fingering across the highest thatched rooftops, then down the stone buildings and across the second-floor shutters where folk still slept. Then sunlight touched the faces of the first-floor shops and the cobbled lanes. A bedroom shutter was pushed open, and a woman in a night dress leaned out. Below, a door opened, and a leather-clad man set a bucket by the stoop. A boy came around a corner leading three fat ewes. Another door opened, shutters were flung back. Pretty soon folk were on the lanes, most of them heading toward the green before the baker's and brewer's shops, arriving to stand in little clusters, staring sky-ward. Soldiers were due this morning. Other soldiers would

be departing. A small flight of winged ones was already rising
into the sky down below Waterpole, but only Meatha from
her height could see it.

On the green now, six young soldiers had gathered to
inspect the bundles laid out on the long tables. Meatha could
feel their tension as if it were her own. The breeze quickened.
She glanced skyward with a sense of excitement, but the first
group of winged ones had gone, and she saw nothing else,
only the deep gray clouds over the eastern hills, still empty of
life. When she turned, sunlight caught across her cheek so the
bones of her face showed sharp and clean, the baby softness
of two years earlier gone now, traded on the training fields
and the battlefields for a taut, quick boyishness that Zephy
said only heightened what she called Meatha's maddening
beauty. Meatha pushed back her dark hair absently.

She knew, without the Seeing, what Zephy would be
feeling this morning, strung taut with the nervy discipline
they had learned, reacting to possible danger—even though
they did not head into battle—with the aggressive eagerness
they had been taught. Zephy, so in charge of herself, so certain about everything. Zephy, so very complete and happy
since she and Thorn had married. Meatha wished she might
have half Zephy's self-assurance and direction, instead of the
emptiness that so often gripped her—instead of the dark fear
that dwelt with her now, stirring a deep subterranean terror
that she did not want to examine.

She needed to talk to someone. Yet that very thought
frightened her. Certainly she could not talk to Zephy this
morning, could not distract her now. Nor could she talk to
Tra. Hoppa without disturbing the old lady's deep concentration over the work in which she was so immersed.

She could talk to Anchorstar if he were here. She swallowed, her own distress replaced suddenly by grief. Where
was Anchorstar? What had happened that day? The sky had
been so clear, their mounts so close together their wings

nearly touched, and Zephy on his other side, Thorn just ahead of him. Anchorstar had looked across at her, his face in the shadow of the mare's wings; and then suddenly he was gone, he and the mare gone as if a hole had opened in the sky.

She saw Anchorstar's lean, leathery face and white hair so vividly she thought for a moment it was a true vision, then knew it was only memory combined with her sharp longing for him. How could he have disappeared? If she could talk with Anchorstar, he could tell her why she had been in the citadel in the middle of the night. He could tell her why she felt such fear.

She wished her Seer's powers could bring him back, that she could bring him to Carriol by the very power of her need for him; but Seer's powers had not been enough, nor had the combined power of all the master council together been enough. Nor had any Seer been able to divine what had happened to him. Though there had been some wild and frightening speculations. Had he been snatched into the unknown lands by some evil they did not understand? Or, as Alardded thought, been thrown by forces even more inexplicable into another time, into the future or the past?

Oh, but that was impossible, that was the stuff of tales or ballads. Like the ballads of Ramad. Not fact. Everyone knew Alardded's ideas could be tinged with madness. Though his inventions were not; they were wonderful. His waterwheels had changed the whole life of Carriol, had made way for goods and luxuries beyond anything they had imagined. And his irrigation network spreading out from the rivers Voda Cul and Somat Cul had brought a richness of pastures and crops never before known across the northern loess plains, so that the fine horses of Carriol had prospered. Yes, Alardded's inventions were solid enough. But his talk of people moving through time was only a flight of his wonderful fancy.

The sun rose higher, and the gray clouds began to

brighten with streaks of reflected light. Then, a sense of flight began to touch her, a sense of freedom, of wild soaring, of wind brushing and twisting past so her heart quickened crazily. She searched the clouds for movement. Below her on the green, folk were all doing the same, staring upward, every Seer sensing flight, every common man taking cue from the Seers, though the winged ones were still invisible in the western sky.

At last she saw tiny specks moving through cloud. She felt their flight, bold and wild and free, as yet unburdened by riders. Her lips moved in silent whisper, she pushed back her dark hair in an impatient gesture, her blood racing at the exhilaration of flight and at the feel of the winged ones' power, at the feel of the wind around them. She thought suddenly of herself as a child again, staring up at the empty sky waiting eagerly and usually futilely for the winged horses of Eresu to appear among cloud. A guilt-ridden child, afraid she would be discovered looking up at the sky. For in Burgdeeth, dreaming of the winged ones had been forbidden. Speaking with them in silence, as she had longed to do, had been punishable by death.

Suddenly the band of flying horses burst out from the cloud, sun slashing across their sweeping wings. They came on fast, soon nearly covered the sky, were dropping down over the pastures in a mass of movement, their silent greetings caressing her. They banked, turned, filled the sky utterly, then plummeted down toward the stable yard and toward the crowded green, a dozen winged ones breaking their flight to land soundlessly and gently among the onlookers, their wings hiding the crowd for a moment in a mass of light-washed movement, amber wings and saffron and gold, snow-pale wings and black. Then they folded their wings across their backs and stood quietly greeting their friends, nuzzling, speaking with voices that came in the Seers' minds in gentle whispers. Meatha saw Zephy with her arms around the neck

of a tall roan mare. Zephy, dressed in flowing green silk like
a real Carriolinian lady; her brown hair, not streaming as
usual, but bound in a coronet braided with gold; gilded boots;
jewelry flashing as she moved so Meatha hardly knew her.
Meatha watched the winged horses crowd around Zephy,
brushing against one another, wings brushing against her like
a benediction. Then Thorn was there, his fighting leathers
new ones, elegant pale hides not yet stained from battle. Soldiers crowded around, the twelve who would ride with them,
other groups of soldiers ready to embark on other missions.
Meatha stared down at her hands on a broken stone wall and
saw that she had gripped until her knuckles were white. She
loosed her fingers, frowning at herself, then watched the
winged ones accept the delicacies the riders had brought
them, knew there would be onyrood pods dipped in honey,
mawzee grain made into cakes with nuts and fruits, new green
shoots from the gardens. She caught the sense of the horses'
pleasure and endearments, the Seers' silent and gentle re-
sponses. And suddenly she wanted to be going too, or to be
flying into battle again in that close brotherhood between Seer
and winged one, leaping down over the heads of earthbound
warriors, her bow taut.

Zephy's and Thorn's flight would end in a descent from
the sky as dramatic and awe-inspiring as riders and horses
together could make it: a descent wrapped in magic, in wonder, in illusion, to impress and so convert their quarry. Ceremony that Meatha knew was not any more to the taste of the
horses of Eresu than it was to Zephy and Thorn. But necessary, if they were to win over the rising cults that had sprung
to life in the coastal countries. If Carriol must win by subter-
fuge, by illusion, then so be it—though the cults were only a
small part of Carriol's problem. For since Meatha and Zephy
and Thorn and Anchorstar, and all that small frightened band
of Children of Ynell had fled the Kubalese caves two years
earlier, Kubal had not only subjugated all of Cloffi, but

seemed intent on defeating and ruling all the coastal countries. On the eastern peninsula, Pelli and Sangur were constantly threatened by raids, though so far they had held their own. In the west, Zandour seemed strong enough, its small council of Seers evidently hardier than the rulers of the central countries. And what was the source of Zandour's power? Did that country indeed still hold a shard of the runestone, as was often whispered? Zandour's Seers claimed they had none such, and many folk believed that when Zandour's leader Hermeth died generations ago, Hermeth's shard of the runestone had disappeared.

If Zandour's Seers did possess a runestone, surely they would not keep it secret from the Seers of Carriol. The power of that stone, wedded to the power of the stone Carriol held, could strengthen both countries considerably against the rise of the Kubalese. Yet where were the other shards of the jade? Meatha wondered. Lost? Buried perhaps, as Carriol's own shard had been buried beneath the city of Burgdeeth? Of the nine shards, Carriol held one, and one was drowned in the sea. Seven were unaccounted for. If we had them all, she thought, and the stone were joined—as Anchorstar dreamed, as Tra. Hoppa dreams when she pours through dusty volumes searching for clues to the disappearance to the shards—if Carriol possessed the whole stone, then we could defeat the Kubalese. She thought with distaste of the piecemeal battles —helping one country, then another—holding impregnable only Carriol. And before Carriol had possessed the one shard of the runestone, she had not been able to do even that, had been able only to defend her own borders, and the refugees who came to her for protection.

Below on the green, four winged ones were being laden with food packs. To see the horses of Eresu wearing pack harness, though it was of their own choosing, so appalled Meatha that she stood staring in dismay for some moments. When she turned away, she was dazzled by the lifting sun.

She stood blinking in the brightness, then at last made her way down between broken stone walls toward the green. She could see Thorn now, his red hair bright against the neck of a white mare.

She shouldered through the crowd to the horses of Eresu, saw a slash of green where Zephy knelt, forgetting her silk gown as she reached to adjust the belly strap around a gray stallion, carefully setting the strap so the pack harness would not chafe him. Zephy, so loving horses ever since she was a tiny girl, when horses were forbidden to them, so close now in her relationship to the winged ones. The stallion's silent voice told her where the strap was uncomfortable. He stretched his dark wings to feel his muscles pull against the harness, then bowed his neck to nuzzle Zephy's shoulder, thanking her. Zephy scratched him under the foreleg with casual familiarity. Zephy, so direct and simple in her relationships—a directness belied now by her elegant clothes, her regal looks, she who cared nothing for clothes. Meatha felt a strange shyness with her suddenly, as if Zephy were a stranger.

Zephy glanced up at her, her brown eyes puzzled as she touched Meatha's unshielded emotions. "What's the matter? You're. . . ."

Meatha blocked her thoughts.

"Is it because I'm got up like this? I'd rather not be!" Then, sensing Meatha's deeper confusion, sensing her distress, she came to Meatha and put her arms around her. "What is it? What's happened to you? Something. . . ." And suddenly Meatha was weeping against Zephy like a child, the darkness engulfing her so it engulfed Zephy, too.

When Meatha calmed at last, Zephy drew away and held her by the shoulders. "Where did such darkness come from? What has happened?" She tried to sort Meatha's thoughts. "Something—last night, so close to you. Something that terrified you. . . ." Zephy swallowed and did not continue for some moments. Then, "It found something within you that made you fear it all the more." She went silent again, sorting. And then with shivering finality,

"You cannot find the shape of what touches you." She swallowed. "Nor—nor can I. Oh Meatha—take care." She studied Meatha. "Maybe you should tell the council. Tell Alardded. . . ." Then suddenly the riders were mounting, Thorn leaping astride a golden stallion, and there was no time to say goodbye. Zephy tried to mount, was caught short in the silken gown. "Blast! I can't do anything in this flaming dress!" Meatha gave her a leg up. Zephy settled her skirt around her, then bent swiftly to touch Meatha's cheek. "It . . . tell someone, Meatha. Tell Alardded. And take care." The gray stallion leaped skyward with a surge of joyful power, following the others, his wings turning the sky to night, then sun slashing across his flanks. Windborne, the winged ones filled the sky; there was a flash of green silk amid the slice of wings, then they were gone in a whirl of color; gone beyond cloud.

A short flight it would be into Pelli, and already plans for their ceremonious descent were sweeping from one mind to another, from rider to horse to the next rider and horse. Meatha felt the messages winging between them even after she could no longer see them; Saw the images they conjured and knew their rising excitement. She stood for some time with her hand raised in farewell, feeling the freedom of their flight; and feeling empty within herself, and lonely.

She turned away at last, awash with loneliness.

That night, again, her dreams trapped and possessed her. She woke more disturbed than the night before and went to her class of seven children so distraught that she made three children cry and spoiled the session for them all. No Seer, child or adult, could deal with a teacher whose mind was in such turmoil. She apologized to them and left them, ashamed, only to find herself weeping in an isolated corner of the tower, terrified by her loss of control, and by the darkness that engulfed her, by the heaviness that gripped her beyond her control.

And more terrifying still, there was a part of her that welcomed that darkness and embraced it.

She must talk to someone, in spite of her reluctance. She must talk to Alardded.

SHE FOUND ALARDDED taking breakfast alone on the green. Usually there was a crowd around him, for his sweeping, unfettered mind and his solid, comforting ways drew men to him. He looked up from a plate of ham pie and charp fruit, watching her approach. He was, Meatha thought, in spite of his sometimes wild ideas, as steady as the great black peaks that rose in the north. As steady—and as unpredictable, too, for Alardded could burst forth with a sudden storming fury just as those peaks could burst forth with fire.

Was he alone now because he had known she was coming to him so distressed? His dark eyes were alert to the small nervous movements of her hands, to the way she stood too stiffly before him. "Sit down, child." His mind examined her blocking with curiosity, and she could not understand why she was blocking. "What brings you to the green so early? Have you had breakfast? Some tea?" He gestured to his small waiter, and the child came running, his long apron flapping around his ankles. She sat stiff and silent, blocking wildly, and puzzled at herself, as young Sheb brought tea. Why was she so reluctant to speak, or to make any vision, so shy and uncomfortable with Alardded? She stared at his sun-browned, wrinkled face and gentle dark eyes and tried to make small talk, but she was not adept at it. Alardded laid a comforting hand on her arm. She was sorry she had come. But why did she block with all her power, a blocking she had perfected in childhood when blocking would save her life—a blocking that now stood as powerful as the master Seer's own skills? Alardded watched her quietly, his own thoughts hidden. Young Sheb returned with fresh-baked bread; Alardded paid him in silver, and he went away happily clinking the coins. Meatha bent her face over her teacup as the darkness of last night again engulfed her.

She had awakened standing in the moonlit citadel, pressing against the stone table, reaching greedily for the runestone; had felt her own lusting greed sharply and suddenly, and had drawn back with a cry, filled with shame. Yet at the same time filled with a desire she could hardly resist to hold and possess the runestone.

Alardded sat quietly waiting for her to ease her mind to him, puzzling at her reluctance, her secrecy. She felt, abstractly, his admiration at the power of her blocking. Then he looked up, and his expression went closed. Hux Tanner was standing behind her chair. She turned to stare up at him, annoyed.

Hux grinned down at her. He did not even feel her anger. His dark beard was sleek and wavy, his grooming perfect as always, to show off the good looks that all the girls admired. Meatha wished he would go away. He must have returned from trading just this morning. He touched her shoulder lightly and sat down beside her, helped himself to Alardded's tea. He had no sense of what had transpired in silence, so filled was he with his own good humor. Alardded rescued his cup, stared absently into its empty depths. "You're back from trading early." The smell of baking filled the air, and they could hear the clatter of pans from the nearby shop. Alardded studied Hux comfortably. "Back in one piece, anyway. You had some close scrapes, Hux. We Saw Kubalese soldiers flanking you several times in visions as sharp as the threat itself. What happened when that large battalion bore down on your wagon just outside Dal? We Saw them and felt the surge of your temper, then nothing. A sense of your horses running, but we could See nothing more, did not know whether you were dead or alive until we touched, much later, a vision of you sprawled before your campfire swilling honeyrot from a Farrian clay jug."

Hux smiled with satisfaction. "I guess my image-changing worked so well that not even you could see me lighting out with that old wagon clattering over the hills." He threw back his head in a huge laugh, his dark hair boiling down over his forehead. "Forty-seven Kubalese raiders chasing after a rock hare thinking it was me, while I drove the wagon, bent-for-Urdd, off in the opposite direction!" He grew serious then. "Kubalese raiders are coming out of the hills everywhere, raiding then gone. Folk travel heavily armed, on the ready for trouble. For the most part, the cities are still able to drive them back. Our raids help to keep the Kubalese down, but there are Seers among the Kubalese, Alardded. Unskilled Seers, but cruel. If we had more than one shard of the runestone, maybe we could thwart those Seers—strengthen our forces enough to destroy the fracking Kubalese! As it is. . . ." He leaned forward. "The stone in the sea, Alardded —if we had one more stone . . ."

Meatha watched Hux now with gentler feelings. She liked him best when he was serious, was concerned for Carriol, angry at Kubalese oppression, the hearty, attentive role dropped—though he seldom used it with her, never with Alardded, of course.

Alardded leaned back in his chair, pushed his plate away. "Perhaps we will have the stone soon. Perhaps. The new diving suit works very well. It is ready for testing in deep waters. The wax-coated leather and lighter metal were just the thing. I plan to take it up to the Bay of Vexin in a few days."

Hux leaned forward eagerly. "I will travel with you, then. I have a cart full of wares to deliver to the charcoal burners and miners, everything imaginable, Zandourian wine, Farrian carved leathers that I had to buy dearly in Dal, boots. I want to see the diving. If the diving suit fit me, Alardded, I would try! Think of it, the stone has lain there for six generations, and only now has anyone known how to bring it up!"

Alardded smiled. "The stone is not in our hands yet, my lad. Though I'll admit I'm excited. It must have been frustrating indeed for our fathers to know where it lay, so deep, to sense it there and not be able to go into those deep waters. But as to the diving . . . ." He gave Hux a wry look. "You won't fit the suit, Hux my boy. You're nearly twice the size of Nicoli or Roth. I'd hate worse than fires in Urdd to have to pull *you* up at the end of the rope!

"But we'd be glad of your company north," he added. "You can help Nicoli with the horses, and I'll be there to protect her from any amorous ideas you might have—though the wily Nicoli can protect herself, certainly. Now show us, Hux, the countries you traveled, and how they fare."

Meatha tried to put her own unsettled emotions aside and attend as Hux showed them in sharp visions the cities of Zandour and Aybil and Farr, the stone and sand fortifications, the patrolling soldiers. He showed them the walled city of Dal, where the dark Seer RilkenDal had reigned before his rule fell to an angry coalition of farmers and sheep men who drove him out of the country keeping only his fine, well-trained mounts. "No one knows where RilkenDal has gone," Hux said. "But all fear him. Fear he will return and retake Dal. Folk seem to want to make a legend of him, which only increases their fear. They speak of him appearing here, there, come out of the sky mounted on a winged one." Hux scowled. "No winged one would carry such as RilkenDal!"

"I would hope not! No winged one would carry a dark Seer!" Alardded said.

They grew silent, lost in speculation. A wagon team passed their table, and the smell of fresh-cut hay filled the air. From a nearby shop the voice of a woman rose, scolding her child, then was still. The young waiter filled their cups.

"However," Alardded said slowly, "there *is* something amiss among the winged ones. They do not speak of it, but a darkness stirs among them. Nicoli senses it. And some of the outlying bands have not been heard of for a long time."

Meatha shivered, was alarmed by Alardded's words; but then, at his mention of darkness, was engulfed in her own confused thoughts once again, so she heard little more of the conversation until suddenly Hux cast into their minds a sharp vision of the place where the cults had gathered along the Pellian coast. She Saw suddenly the mass of hide tents and lean-tos clustered above the sea cliff, and she could imagine Zephy and Thorn and their companions there now, making impressive ceremony for the gathered cultists. Hux showed them the cultist's passive faces, their quiet submissive minds, so very puzzling.

"They swear hatred of the Kubalese raiders," Hux said, "but they will not attack them, even to save other cultists. There is—there is a leader who guides the cult leaders, but I can get little sense of him—or of *her*. Sometimes I think it is a woman. Someone they think of nearly as a god. The cults are so. . . ."

"Yes. So committed to good," Alardded said, "yet so unwilling to uphold that commitment." Then, "We have known nothing of such a leader. We must speak in Council of it. We must speak with the missions that have gone out. If Zephy and Thorn and the other missions can learn something of an unknown leader . . ."

Hux nodded. "Perhaps, in the journal I bargained for in Zandour and carried hidden in my tunic, there might be some answer to the puzzle. It is written by a Zandourian soldier and covers many years up to the present—but a rambling, incomplete history and hard to read. Handwriting worse than my own." He showed them in vision the small leather-bound volume he had given to Tra. Hoppa at first light, going directly to her chambers from unhitching and tending his horses. They felt Tra. Hoppa's excitement as she stood in the doorway, her white hair ruffled from sleep, and took the little book in her thin hands, then eagerly turned the pages. Felt her disappointment at the scratchy, illegible script. But the old woman's eyes had filled with hope nonetheless, hope that with patient deciphering the cults might be explained, or, even more important, some clue to the missing shards of the runestone might be found.

The sea wind quickened up along the cliff, lifting the tall grass that grew between the broken old walls, then slicing down into the town. On the cobbled street beside the green a line of carts drew up and began to unload vegetables and bags of grain and flour and bolts of cloth from the north of Carriol and to load up ale kegs and hides and small parcels. Along the upper-story living quarters above the shops, curtains blew in and out between the shutters. A band of children raced by on their way to some lesson or perhaps to weapons practice. Their small waiter hastily filled the tea mugs, then removed his apron and vanished, following his peers. More wagons rumbled in. Smoke from chimneys rose then was snatched away by the wind.

A band of soldiers rode by toward the upper practice grounds, then the sense of skyward motion gripped them all, and every Seer looked up into the western sky, their gazes copied at once by every common man; and soon out of the sky came winging a battalion of returning riders, sunlight slanting across their armor. The sense of them said plainly they had been victorious—but that they carried two dead. All the town turned at once to preparing the simple ritual that would pre-cede the burial of the dead. Alardded and Hux and Meatha began to clear away the tables so the green could be more easily used for the parting ceremony; then Alardded went alone to the citadel, where his powers would be stronger, to tell, across the length of Carriol, of the deaths.

Meatha watched the bodies lifted gently from the backs of the winged ones and laid out in the simple pine caskets kept always ready for such deaths. She shivered and felt sick and turned away.

But why should these deaths upset her? She had seen dead soldiers. These were boys from the north of Carriol, farm boys, one as freckled as an otero egg, with tumbled sandy hair. She had danced with him once at a festival. Death, and the fear of death, filled and sickened her.

She did not sleep well that night, and the next morning was tired and irritable and filled with formless fears. And with that presence, cold and foreboding, that she could not escape nor name, and to which her spirit seemed to cling in spite of fear.

Chapter
Three

SHORREN PAUSED on a narrow ledge well down in the abyss, then her coat blazed white as she leaped deeper still, to join Lobon. *Something more than Dracvadrig stirs in this pit, Lobon. Something I cannot yet name or put form to.*

"*I* sense it, Shorren! Don't you think I sense it!"

The two dog wolves followed Shorren, to press around Lobon as he descended between jagged boulders.

They had been four days in the abyss, yet seemed hardly to have broken away from its rim, so twisting and slow was the route, so deep the chasm. And Lobon had begun to swing from anger to a deep depression that would grip him for hours as Dracvadrig sought to control his mind.

Why didn't Dracvadrig simply come out of the abyss and battle him for the four stones he carried, for the added power they would bring? Why didn't the dragon attack him, show itself, instead of waiting unseen, reaching up only with mind-powers to haze and confuse him! To enervate his will with darkness and with tricks. Twice the wolves had driven back fire ogres before he even knew they were there, so dulled had he become, and once a huge, coiling macadach, whose poisonous bite would have killed him. Sometimes he was aware of little else but the creeping darkness freezing his thoughts; he knew he must find Dracvadrig soon, before he was weakened further. And now the sense of other beings assailed them, too, of an evil creature as cold-blodded as the macadach, though he could not make out what it was.

They came at midmorning to a lava river twisting between jagged monoliths of stone and stood considering how to cross. When the earth trembled beneath them, Lobon shrugged. What danger could the earth present, that Dracvadrig could not? Moving slowly, heavily, with Dracvadrig's power on him, he found boulders small enough to roll down the cliff into the lava river and began to construct a way across.

It took the better part of the day to make a causeway they could cross without being scalded by the flowing lava. The heat was unbearable; Lobon's leathers were soaked with sweat, the wolves panting. Yet they must cross the lava, for he could sense Dracvadrig far deeper in the abyss. Once across, Lobon's strength was drained. He rested between stone outcroppings where a small trickle of hot water came down. He drank and filled the waterskin. The air was heavy with smoke and unfamiliar fumes. Even the wolves' strength had ebbed. They all slept fitfully through a red-tinged darkness and moved on again in a sulfurous dawn, pushed deeper and deeper into the abyss, across more molten rivers and nearly impassable rifts. They ate lizards and rock crabs and snakes and had never enough to drink. All four sensed that they were watched by the firemaster, though he was never there. Nor did he speak again. The wolves were increasingly edgy. Lobon was driven on, despite his strange confusion and fatigue, by his all-consuming need to kill Dracvadrig.

Sometimes he would feel Dracvadrig turn from him and reach out for the girl, and then he would come more fully alert, and would follow the creature's mind and watch him lay his ugly darkness on her thoughts. He would watch Dracvadrig lead her to Carriol's citadel again and again, watch her stand staring mesmerized at the suspended runestone, then turn away as Dracvadrig built a need in her to hold the stone that at last she would be unable to resist. Her desire for it was beginning to consume her like a slow fire, and soon, Lobon knew, she must burst the bonds of her own reticence. Dracvadrig seemed in no hurry, as if he were enjoying her torment.

As he is enjoying mine? Lobon thought. Is that why he does not attack me for the stones, but leads me always deeper into the abyss? He stared down into the pit that humped and curved below him, seeming to go on forever.

"Curse him. Curse his burning soul. Why doesn't he show himself, come up here and face us and *see* who is the more powerful!"

Shorren stared up at him, her yellow eyes steady. *You are letting him goad you, Lobon. You faint at shadows.*

"Dracvadrig is no shadow!"

You let the firemaster destroy your temper. You make yourself weary sparring with what is not yet known.

He laid a hand on her heavy white coat, felt the power of her muscles, the breadth of her shoulders. He wished she would be still. He wanted to confront Dracvadrig, to battle Dracvadrig! Couldn't she understand that!

All four of us seek the same goal, she said calmly, infuriating him further. *We all seek Dracvadrig's death and the joining of the stone. We all seek the salvation of Ere.*

He turned to glare at her. "*I* seek only to kill the worm Dracvadrig! To avenge my father's death! The saving of Ere is not my business, nor is the joining of the stone!"

Shorren's eyes slitted. *The saving of Ere had better be your business, Lobon the hotheaded. It is not enough simply to kill Dracvadrig. The powers within you were born to the salvation of Ere, through your father's blood. If you do not seek to save Ere, you do not avenge Ramad's death, you defile it.*

"I will avenge my father's death in the killing of Dracvadrig."

You do not see clearly. The bitch wolf's ears were flat, her lips curled back over gleaming teeth. *Your hatred warps your senses, Lobon, son of Ramad! If you deny Ramad's quest, not only do you refuse to avenge him, but you deny the rebirth of your own soul. You fail the purpose of your own life. You will die unable to be born anew. Or you will neither die nor be reborn, but lie in limbo as does Cadach who cannot die, who stands forever locked into the trunk of a tree in the caves of Owdneet.*

"*I* don't care about my soul! And the tale of Cadach is nothing but an old woman's tale!"

It is not, Lobon. Cadach lives. Your own mother spoke with him when she came into Owdneet's caves searching for a way into Time, seeking to follow Ramad into Time. And Cadach's white-haired children live, atoning for him again and again through all of Time. Know you, whelp, that the woman Gredillon who raised your father was one of Cadach's white-haired children, as was Anchorstar, who helped your father save one shard of the runestone and acquire another. Never think, Lobon the big-headed, that Cadach is a myth—or that such could not happen to you!

"Well, but Cadach—"

Cadach denied his heritage and sold his soul for avarice and greed —in your own time, Lobon, in this time, before he was swept back in Time to die a living death in the tree, never to know the progression of his soul.

Lobon scowled. He did not want to believe in Cadach. He was not sure he believed in the progression of souls. Such things were a nuisance to think about.

The two dog wolves raised their muzzles and stared at him with hard yellow eyes. Crieba said, *Shorren is right, you are guardian of more than you are willing to embrace, Lobon. You lust for revenge alone, and that is not enough, even in the name of your father. You shame Ramad.*

Lobon turned from them, furious, and swung away down the cliff. His own mother had said those same words before he left the house of Canoldir, told him that he shamed his father's name with his self-centered fury. "You must temper the purpose that leads you into battle before you will be equal to Ram! As you are now, Lobon, you are not fit to hold the fate of Ere in your hands!"

He had shouted, "I don't care about Ere! I care only to avenge Ramad!"

"Then you are not man enough to be Ramad's son! You will leave this house without *my* blessing, and without Canoldir's blessing!"

He had not spoken to her again, had gone out of the house of Canoldir in a rage, the three wolves leaping to join him unbidden. He had found his way down the ice mountains, warmed by his own terrible anger, had come at last to the lands where Time flowed forward like a river, had crossed the mountains to the range below the glacier, driven by rage and by the sense of the runestone there coupled with the sense of Dracvadrig, and never once had he thought or cared that he could not even have left Canoldir's house without that man willing him back into the mainstream of Time.

The wolves had censured him constantly for his temper. "And why," he said now, scowling, "why, Shorren the wise, why does Dracvadrig seek out that one stone in Carriol, when the four stones *I* carry are so much nearer to hand? Answer me *that* riddle!"

Dracvadrig thinks to have your stones easily enough. He considers them already in his hand, to be plucked when he is ready. He is most pleased that you bring them closer to him with each step we take. Dracvadrig lusts after the more unattainable stone—that stone that hangs in Carriol. And he wants, also, the stone that lies in the sea. Shorren stretched and stared down at the broken crevices below them, then looked back at Lobon. Her white coat caught the slanting light. *You, Lobon, he considers but a plaything. If you knew Dracvadrig as you should, you would see him taking the form of the dragon simply for the pleasure of catching a fire ogre and tossing it, teasing it, letting it run, then snatching it up and, much later, killing it. Just so does he play with us, just so does he watch us descend to him, just so does he send fire ogres and serpents to harass us.*

"Why do you remain with me, then?" he said sarcasti-
cally. "And how do you know more of Dracvadrig than I,
bitch wolf?"

*We follow because we must. We are linked to Ramad just as you
are. And we know Dracvadrig because we attend to the subleties of
his presence, Lobon, while your mind is fogged by his thoughts, and by
your fury, and by your preoccupation with the girl.*

"The girl could be useful! You don't—"

*Useful to you in gaining revenge. Not useful in preventing
Dracvadrig from having Carriol's stone. Not useful for the good of
Ere.*

"You talk drivel! Revenge is all that is needed." He was
sick to death of her censure. He snatched the wolf bell from
his tunic. "All three of you talk rubbish." He stared at them
in fury, his dark eyes flashing, his unruly red hair gone wil-
der, as if the very power of his anger made it flame. He hated
the wolves in that moment. They were arrogant, filled with
senseless dreams. They did not understand or care how he
felt. He didn't need them; he would be better off without
their haranguing. He raised the wolf bell and brought a power
to banish them, to drive them away. Let them return to Skeelie and the rest of their cursed band. "You will—"

A black streak leaped, Feldyn's teeth gripped his arm,
Feldyn's weight crashed into him. He went down, the black
wolf's teeth inches from his face, Crieba and Shorren crowd-
ing over him. He could feel their breath, see nothing but
killer's teeth. He stared up at them unbelieving. Never had
the wolves acted so, never. He was their master. He was
master of the wolf bell.

Feldyn's thought came sharp: *You are not our master,
Lobon! Not as Ramad was, though you hold the wolf bell. You have
not Ramad's level of power, or his caring, yet to master us. You are
our brother, yes. And because you are, we speak truths to you, and
we command that you listen to us!*

Crieba's voice was cold behind his silver snarl. *The great
wolves have power of their own, Lobon! You will not banish us. This*

mission is ours as much as it is yours. Our sire died by Ramad's side battling Dracvadrig, and we too will avenge. But there is more to avenging, Lobon the hot-tempered, than you are willing to admit. You will fail, Lobon. You will ultimately fail unless you accept the whole of Ramad's commitment, as do we; unless you strive to win that which Ramad himself would win.

The wolves turned away from him then and left him sprawled. *You can stay or follow us*, Shorren said, *just as you choose.*

He stared after their retreating backsides. Their tails swung jauntily. He looked down at the wolf bell clutched in his sweating hand. His fury was spent, his doubts painful and raw. He cursed them silently and ground his fist against the wolf bell.

He rose at last and started on. They could die in the blasted pit for all of him. He would seek Dracvadrig alone.

IN A LAND OF ICE that lay beyond Time, in a villa walled by banks of snow, a woman watched in sharp vision Lobon's rude and foolish defiance of the wolves. When she let the vision go at last, she stood staring into the cold ashes of the fireplace, her fist pushing against the stone mantel in a gesture very like Lobon's. A tall woman, thin, inclined to stand stooped unless she remembered and straightened. The knot of her dark hair was half-undone, twisted over her shoulder. Lines of care and loss creased her face. She was alone in the raftered hall, for Canoldir was hunting far back in the ice mountains; though even at such a distance he touched her now and again with a warmth that helped to ease her distress. The seven wolves who hunted with him touched her mind too, whispering now, *Sister, be of cheer, sister of wolves. We tell you that not Shorren nor Feldyn nor Crieba will leave Lobon. They will see him safe, in spite of his surly ways.*

But their assurance did little good. Skeelie worried for Lobon and was furious with him. She turned away from the mantel at last, her light fur robe swirling around her long legs, and began to pace the room. She was a woman bred to sword and saddle, she carried the difficult years well, as trim and agile as she had ever been. She seemed self-contained, but the younger, vulnerable Skeelie was there, the distress and love she had felt for Ram ever since she was a child pouring out now over his son to leave her shaken. What had she done or failed to do, that Lobon should grow to manhood with such shortsighted purpose?

He will grow out of it, Canoldir whispered to her, touching her mind from afar. *Ramad's blood is in him, and your own blood, my love. Lobon will come through, to be what he was meant to be.*

She bowed her head, warm in Canoldir's gentleness; but she knew she had failed Lobon. Had she not expected enough of Lobon the child? Not loved him strongly enough? Not praised him enough for successes and been strong enough with him about failures? Eresu knew, she had tried to be a gentle mother, yet give him the strength that Ramad would have given.

Since they had come to Canoldir when Lobon was eight, fleeing from the city of cones, Canoldir had been as strong and fair a father as Ramad himself would have been. Where then did that wild angry streak in Lobon come from? Certainly not from Canoldir's treatment. And not, alone, from the child's memory of his father's death, she knew.

For Lobon's anger had shown itself much earlier than Ram's death, from the time he was a small babe *demanding* to be fed, *demanding* to be comforted, never asking or gentle. Ramad had laughed at—and wondered at—the child's temperament. And frowned, disturbed, sometimes. For Lobon was too much like Ramad's mother. He was, Skeelie admitted, far too much like Tayba, who had conceived Ramad out of angry defiance, borne him in anger, and nearly killed him when he was nine because of her own willful and traitorous

greed. Tayba, who with her fiery temperament had been one
cause of the violent clashing of evil against good that had
shattered the runestone of Eresu there on Tala-charen. Yes,
surely Tayba's violent spirit was mirrored in her grandson.
Could I not, Skeelie thought, could I not have prevented
Lobon's gowing up to be what he is?

You could not have! Canoldir's thoughts shouted in her
mind like a roaring bear, making her smile. She let her burden
relax a little, warmed by him, and paused from her pacing
beside a low table near the hearth.

At last she sat down on a hide-covered cushion before the
table and took up quill and ink. She sat thinking for a while
longer, letting her mind ease, putting herself into a routine of
discipline that had been hard to learn, yet necessary to her
survival against the madness that had seemed to hold her after
Ram's death.

She had lost the first pages of the journal long ago, had
left them, she supposed, in the city of cones. The memory of
those days after Ram died was so twisted and painful that
even now her thoughts, straying to that time, were like an
open wound. She had never stopped loving Ram and never
would, though she loved Canoldir too in another way, with
another part of herself. Canoldir knew it. He sheltered her
and soothed her, and took joy in her in spite of her commitment to Ram. She filled the page slowly, released at last of
some of her distress over Lobon, then laid down her pen and
sat looking into the cold fireplace. Suddenly she felt the stirring movement of the earth near to Lobon, and tensed anew.
When it continued unabated, she reached out to Canoldir,
frightened. *The land trembles, Canoldir! The land in that time
trembles steadily beneath the chasm, it—*

*Yes, the land trembles. I cannot stay it, Skeelie. Even the
Luff'Eresi cannot stay such a thing as that.*

"*But you—*"

You know what is happening to my powers, you know I do not reach out of Time as well as once I did, that I cannot snatch Lobon from danger! Nor should I!

"*Because of me, your powers—*"

We do not know that. Whatever it is, I cannot deal with fate as if it were a game. She felt his anger and turned away from him in her mind until he should calm. She did not like to distress him like this.

But she could not help her own distress. She had felt for some time that forces across Ere she could not sort out or describe were drawing together, insidious and threatening. Forces very aware of Lobon and utterly unpredictable as they moved toward him. Forces at least as powerful as those that had swept around her and Ram before the runestone split. Forces that could bring, now, even more disaster?

HIGH IN THE BLACK CLIFF overlooking the abyss, one small portal might be seen, if the shadows lay right. One would not expect a portal there. It was like a single eye in the smooth stone wall, black against black. It looked out from a room carved deep in the living stone, a dim room, square and rough-hewn. A thin figure moved inside, so pale it seemed to cast its own light. It stood looking out the portal, so the hole held a smear of white as if the eye had opened wide. The figure was still, then turned at last to look back into the room behind her where two men sat, one at either end of a stone bench carved along the back wall. Her voice was flat, cold. "Light the lamp, Dracvadrig."

The man grunted. Flint sparked, sparked again, then a flame flared and settled at last into a greasy glow smelling of lamb fat. It threw Dracvadrig's tall thin shadow up the wall in such a way that he might have been in dragon form still, rearing up the wall. When he leaned across the lamp, it cast an eerie light up over his long, lined face, picking out warty skin as if the dragon in him never truly abated and making the large high-bridged nose seem huge. His eyes were the color of mud. His lank hair would take on life only when it became wattled dragon mane. His fingers and nails were long and brown and looked as if they could grow into claws with ease. His voice was dry and harsh, little different from when he took dragon form, only not as loud. He sat stiffly against the cave wall, as if he were not entirely comfortable in human form. "Something touches this Lobon, something I don't like," he said. "Another Seer touches him. Perhaps more than one Seer. I don't—"

"I feel it," RilkenDal said, cutting him short. He sat more easily than Dracvadrig. He had laid his sword on the bench between them and played now with the leather thong attached to the hilt. He was a broad, heavy Seer with greasy black hair, as dark of countenance as the ancestors whose names he bore and with a mind perhaps darker. "Yes. A female Seer touches him." He glanced at the pale woman. "What female, Kish? What is she up to?"

"Whoever she is, we don't need her," Kish said. Her eyes were lidless, like serpent's eyes. Her pale skin caught the dim lamplight like the white belly-skin of a snake. But her body was voluptuous, and she could be beautiful when she chose —at least to a man with jaded tastes. Now she was only cold, bored with her companions and showing it.

"It is a presence I cannot abide," Dracvadrig said. "If it is female, Kish, then *you* must deal with it."

Kish's laugh was cold as winter. "What harm can she do? The boy is too filled with anger to master any sublety of power, even with the help of another Seer."

RilkenDal shifted his weight and belched. "You speak of sublety, Kish, as if you understood the word."

She gave him a look he could interpret any way he chose. Dracvadrig retreated into the trancelike state where he touched Lobon's mind most easily. The other two watched him, then reached out with their thoughts to enter his mind as fluttering moths might enter a path of dulled light. Together the three observed Lobon working deeper into the pit, saw him ever following the false sense of Dracvadrig that the firemaster had laid for him. They saw he was alone, that the wolves moved elsewhere along the rim of the smoke-filled chasm. "He believes you are down there," Kish said, pleased. "When he reaches the nether levels and comes to the dungeons. . . ."

"Yes. Then he will know what Urdd is." Dracvadrig smiled. "And he will know what we intend for him."

"Not all that we intend," she said, stretching her long body pleasurably, then flowing down on the bench beside him in one sinuous movement.

"No." Dracvadrig smiled. "Not until we bring the girl. He should like that well enough." He moved closer to Kish, as if the turn of their thoughts inspired him.

"He will come to the gates tonight," she said, laying her cold hand carelessly on his knee. "The wolves will soon know the gate is there. They—well but the boy and the wolves have quarreled. Still, I wish they would go away." She glanced at Dracvadrig. "I wish you would kill the wolves, I don't like them. Dragons can eat wolves."

Dracvadrig did not answer. He had abandoned Lobon and moved into the mind of the girl, manipulating her thoughts, casting the runestone's image sharp across her desires. He stayed with her, prodding her, for the rest of the afternoon, stayed with her until she went to her bed at last, shortly after supper.

SHE WAS SO TIRED, sick with exhaustion, was asleep almost before she had pulled up the covers. She cried out once in her sleep, but she could not push the darkness away. The dark was warm and comforting, and she could not bring herself to awaken. She began to cleave to it, soon was resting gently against it.

She woke to early dawn. Sea light rippled across her

stone ceiling. Her head was filled with a muddle of facts that startled her, with details of the talents of Carriol's Seers as if their personal habits at plying their skills were important to her; with the details of Alardded's diving suit and with his plans for bringing up the lost stone. Why had she marshaled such knowledge? What had she dreamed, to dredge up such facts? And over it all lay the image of the runestone, clear and bright and beguiling.

She had begun to think of the stone as her stone. After all, it was she and Zephy who had found it hidden in the tunnel in Burgdeeth. It was she who had hidden it in the donkey saddle, to get it out of Cloffi in safety. She turned over and pulled the blankets up. Despite the strange thoughts that filled her mind, she felt rested. Calm and strong and— excited. Her whole being anticipated something wonderful. Something yet to be revealed to her.

She could hear the movement of horses below in the town and the voices of men and women starting the day. Then she heard a nicker from high within the tower and knew that a band of winged ones had come together in the citadel in some gentle and private ceremony—perhaps before departing for battle. The citadel had been theirs long before it was man's, long before Carriol's Seers gathered there. Below, the rattle of cart wheels struck across cobbles, a heavy wagon, probably iron ore or grain. She rose at last. The odor of frying mawzee cakes came from the kitchens. She began to dress, hungry suddenly; very sure of herself, very calm despite the eager anticipation that welled deep within, that made her heart pound; but that must be pushed back now, and hidden.

Chapter
Four

ZEPHY TUGGED at the gold band woven into her hair, loosed the braid and let it fall, then began to unbraid it. Her head itched, she disliked her hair done up so and needed badly to brush it. She sat cross-legged in their tent, Thorn lying stretched out beside her, already snoring. She turned the lampwick down to a dull glow. She was so tired even her arms ached as she brushed, so weary from days of creating visions to add wonder and glamour to their every simple task, of surrounding their treatment of the sick with magical incantations, even of accompanying the doctoring by Carriol's true healer, Nebben, with added ceremonies. All meaningless, but all creating wonder in simple minds, presenting to the cults an aura of magic and power like a golden cloak to heighten even further Carriol's reputation of strength. The cults must come to believe in Carriol's Seers utterly, must be awed by Carriol to the extent that at last they would speak freely of their warrior queen, she who lurked so mysteriously in the background. None would speak of her, even think of her except in involuntary fleeting shadows, vague darkness gone at once, without image.

Zephy sighed. They must learn the nature of this leader, for in her lay the true nature of the cults. So much deception, so much secrecy. Why? And now there was the worry over Meatha to nag at her, to try her own loyalties unbearably.

Meatha, caught in some mysterious and urgent mission that she completely blocked from them. Why would she block? What secret need she keep? Meatha, closer to her than any sister could be. She knew she could not give up her trust in Meatha, despite her unease; at least for a little while. That she must give Meatha time to prove herself. And then tonight, such a sharp vision of Meatha standing on the cliff among the ruins calling out in the darkness, speaking across the mountains to the mare Michennann. Why such secrecy? She had blocked furiously as she called. What did Meatha plan, what did she intend? Stealth was not natural to Meatha.

Thorn woke with the turmoil of her thoughts. He sat up and touched her hair, felt her distress as his own, took her face in his hands and studied her, then touched the frown between her brows with a gentle finger. "It will come right, Zephy. Perhaps your unease is for nothing. Though—though no one knows Meatha better than you."

"What is she doing? Why is she so upset, so secret? What is so urgent? Why does she call the mare now? Why does she block me so I can't speak with her?"

He put his arm around her, drew her close.

"And why does she block from the council, Thorn? Why?" She looked up at him in the dim lamplight. "I know I should speak to the council. But I can't. At least—not yet." She blew out the lamp. They heard the horses stir once above the pounding of the sea. She must trust in Meatha, she must have faith in Meatha. She could not abandon their friendship so lightly.

MEATHA WENT TO SLEEP at last. She was not at all sure the mare would come, was puzzled at her reluctance. They were close, they had fought battles together. What was the matter with Michennann? She could not forsake her now, Michennann who, above all the winged ones, could be trusted in this.

She must call Michennann again and again, until it was settled.

She woke at first light to return to the cliff and renew her call across half of Ere to where the gray mare grazed. She felt Michennann's resistance again, was hurt by it; but she pressed stubbornly on until at last she felt the mare soften. Then Meatha drew away and let the mare be, to dwell on it, to come gently to terms with it as was Michennann's way. She looked across the narrow sea channel to the isle of Fentress. Dawn touched the weathered cottages, and already half a dozen children had run out to scurry along the rocky shore with clam buckets, laughing and playing at tag before they settled to their morning's work. She could not remember playing so as a child. In Burgdeeth, little girls were not encouraged to play. She left the cliff at last, eager to lose herself in her own morning's work, and when she reached Tra. Hoppa's chambers she found the old lady already seated at her table with the small leather-bound book Hux had brought open in front of her. Sea light played through the open window across Tra. Hoppa's white hair, and a breeze stirred the pages over which she scowled. "It's like hen scratching. I can make out so little." The old lady's thin fingers traced the nearly illegible text.

"But you've made notes," Meatha said, looking down over her shoulder.

"I've made notes from the first part. That's easier to read because it tells of what we already know. It speaks of Ramad of the wolves as a small child, battling the dark Seer Har-Thass. It tells how Ramad killed the gantroed atop Talacharen, and how the forces spun around him so violently they cracked open the mountain and split the stone into nine shards. Then it tells how Ramad in later years battled the shape-changer Hape, clinging to its back as it flew over the sea, how the Hape dove into the sea and nearly drowned Ramad, and the runestone was lost. How Ramad and his

49

companions burned the castle of Hape, and only one dark Seer escaped them. But then—do you remember the words Ramad's mother wrote in the Book of Carriol soon after that battle?

"How could I forget? Tayba of Carriol wrote, *Ramad is gone. The battle of Hape is ended and Ram is gone, I fear forever, from this place.* I've never understood what she meant. Gone where? She can't have meant that he died. There are tales of Ramad in later years, defeating NilokEm at the dark tower. And why would he go away forever from Carriol? But still, there is nothing more in her journal. The rest of the pages are blank." Meatha looked at Tra. Hoppa, puzzling, then caught the faint sense of the old woman's excitement. "What does *this* book say?"

"That Ramad carried another runestone," the old lady said. "That after his shard of the runestone was lost in the sea, he came into possession of another—but then the book becomes muddled, for what I think it's saying is not possible."

Meatha studied the scrawling handwriting and could make out only a few words. Ramad's name was repeated several times, making her feel strange, though she could not understand why. Tra. Hoppa followed the words with her finger, as if touching them would make them more legible. At last she sat back in exasperation. "Make us some tea, Meatha. All of this is so difficult. It makes no sense at all. It seems—there are parts of it that are like the ballad of Hermeth, and that simply adds to the puzzle."

Meatha made the tea, replaced the tin kettle on the back of the clay stove, and found some seed cakes in a crock. When she returned to the table with the tray, Tra. Hoppa looked strange. "I've made out a few lines more," she said, frowning. "But—what can it mean? I always thought the ballad of Hermeth was myth, embroidered from some incident long ago twisted out of its original shape. But perhaps. . . ." She settled back, sipping the welcome tea. "Meatha, this book tells the same tale as the ballad, copied from an old, old manuscript. It tells of NilokEm and Ramad fighting beside the dark tower nine years after the battle of Hape—we have always known that NilokEm was killed in that battle. But now—this says that Hermeth of Zandour fought beside Ramad in that battle. Hermeth—who was not yet born. It says then that when Hermeth fought in that same dark wood eighty years later, it was the *same* battle. That the two battles were one. That men fighting in that later battle saw Ramad there, surrounded by wolves, fighting by Hermeth's side. A young Ramad, no older than Hermeth himself." She looked up at Meatha, her blue eyes lit with puzzled excitement. "What have we found, Meatha? Can we believe these words? That Ramad. . . ."

"That Ramad moved through Time," Meatha whispered, "just as the ballad says. That—that the ballad speaks truly." She stared at Tra. Hoppa, shook her head uncertainly.

Tra. Hoppa rose and began to pace, slim and quick, her coarsespun gown whirling around her sandaled feet. She paused at last beside the window to stare down at the sea, and when she turned back, her face held that look of stubborn determination that both Meatha and Zephy knew so well. "Meatha, could you . . ." but her voice died, she clutched at the sill as the tower was jolted by earthshock. Meatha caught the cups before they slid to the floor.

It was only an instant, dizzying them. Then the tremor was past. They looked at one another, trying to put down their fear, for fear of the erupting earth was a powerful force in Ere's heritage—fear of the Ring of Fire, whose eruptions had shaped men's lives since times long, long forgotten. Quickly Meatha reached out to Carriol's other Seers, felt them join and exchange their experiences of the tremor, and finally she relaxed. "It was only a small local one; there was hardly a shudder in the north."

Tra. Hoppa nodded, took up her question as if nothing

had happened. "Could you read more of the book through the power of Seeing? Could you decipher these pages with the Seeing?"

"I don't—I've never tried such a thing." And again a strange unease gripped her. "A stronger Seer could, perhaps, a master Seer. . . ."

"There is more power in you than you know, child. Hux tried, when he bought the book from the little gutter lady in Zandour, but he—Hux's skills run more to charming young women into his wagon than to such subtleties as taking the meaning direct from the pages of a book."

Meatha grinned. Hux's success with women was as much a part of Carriol as was fair day or the novice games. Hesitantly she picked up the little book of loosely bound pages. Wind rifled the parchment sheets, then was still. She touched the script delicately, as if she touched a living thing. Reluctantly, and then with growing excitement, she tried to encompass the pages with all of her being, to encompass the sense of the writer as if she were one with him.

After a few moments she began to feel unusually warm. Her hands began to tingle. Then came strange smells, the dry, dusty smell of old wood, the smell of drying hay, then the shadowy sense of a small room, a wooden shed. Slowly she felt herself possessed by another who leaned over parchment, writing. The outlines of Tra. Hoppa's room had faded until only shadows remained. Words were forming in her mind in dark flashes. An allusion to Time, to warriors— *"Come together out of two different times!"* She whispered, "Yes, Ramad!" and she didn't know who she was speaking to. "Ramad came forward in Time." She felt the shock of this— and the truth of it. The scenes of battle were sharp. The scenes of Zandour itself rang true for her. Her voice shook. "Hermeth gave to Ramad the runestone." She felt as if *she* were writing the words. "Hermeth gave him the stone that had passed down from Hermeth's great-grandfather who was NilokEm." She spoke on, not even looking at the pages. "And

Ramad carried a second stone taken from his true love, taken from. . . ." but the words were fading in her mind now as a voice fades. Soon only the sense of some terrible grief remained with her.

She came awake in Tra. Hoppa's room, stood staring at the old lady in confusion.

Then she said softly, and with infinite sadness, "Ramad hit Telien and took the stone from her. And Telien vanished from that Time and that place. . . ." She was shaking, felt cold and sick. "And Ramad wept," she said. And she was weeping, too. Tears poured down uncontrollably; shuddering sobs shook her. Tra. Hoppa gathered her in. Meatha wept against the old lady's shoulder until at last she was spent, shivering with anguish and cold.

"Come child, you need rest. More than this vision alone is bothering you."

She shook her head. "I can't—"

"Come. I know you have not slept well. You do not look well. I saw you out early this morning. I saw you pacing the cliff the night before Zephy and Thorn left, in the cold wind with only that light cloak. Come, you can miss weapons practice for one day." The old woman took her hand in a strong grip and led her from the room and down the stone stairs to her own room, where she kindled a fire, then called one of the girls whose turn it was to serve to fill a hot tub. When the jugs had been brought and the tub was steaming, Tra. Hoppa helped Meatha to bathe, to warm herself, then got her into her narrow little bed and covered her up warm. Meatha, torn with a storm of emotions, did not resist. Tra. Hoppa drew another blanket close, where she could reach it. "You are sickening for something. You must rest." The old woman, without Seer's skills, could only see the surface of her distress. "Try to sleep, I'll see that an early noon meal is brought."

"But I must—it isn't even the middle of the day, I can't. . . ."

"Do as I say. Your morning's work belongs to me, and I

direct you to stay in bed. I will send a message that you will not appear at weapons practice. And Bernaden will take your class of children." Tra. Hoppa touched her cheek lightly, more worried than she wanted to show, and left her. Meatha lay staring at her ceiling, numb and confused, not wanting to think, yet unable to stop thinking.

Why was something deep within her frightened by the tale of Ramad? Why were her new, exciting powers shaken by that tale? Oh, but those powers could not be shaken. They could not. Too much depended on her. Too much—she was so drowsy, relaxed at last, the revulsion and fear fading, not really important. . . . One thing was important, one thing. The mission she would accomplish for Ere. Nothing, no imagined fear, could change that.

Was she asleep when the image came? She jerked upright and sat staring around her, not seeing her room but instead a deep chasm and a fiery river running between jagged cliffs, the sky heavy with smoke. She felt a presence, but she saw no one at first, only after a moment became aware of a wolf, gray against gray stone, watching her. Then she saw in the dark shadows beside him a second wolf black as night. They were terrifyingly beautiful, both staring at her with eyes as golden as Ere's moons. She could feel the intricacies of their minds probing her thoughts delicately. She quailed before their stares, before the touch of those minds. But suddenly they turned and vanished, and in their place stood a tall young man with tangled red hair, every color of red, and eyes black and fierce. He seemed so angry, had the look of an animal, predatory as wolves, half ready to attack something—but half at bay, too. And she thought, with a burning purpose eating at him, a cold unshakable purpose—not unlike her own. She wanted to reach out, to speak to him. Something prevented her. She crouched on her bed not seeing her room, trapped by the seething abyss and by the sense of him wild and appealing. And then the force she knew so well blurred her mind, and she closed her eyes and knew nothing more of him.

She woke to noon sun flooding her room. A girl stood with her back to her, placing a tray by the bed.

"Clytey?"

Clytey turned. "Tra. Hoppa said you were sick. Too sick for company? I brought enough for two, but. . . ." The younger girl hesitated.

Meatha was muzzy from sleep. She tried to smile. The scent of tammi tea and of broiled scallops brought her more fully awake. She found suddenly that she was ravenous. She sat up, tried to clear her mind, to clear away shadows. A sense of excitement lingered, a sense of power she did not want Clytey to see. Blocking, smiling at last, she gestured for Clytey to sit down.

Clytey shook her sandy hair away from her cheek and pulled up a stool. "You are pale, you. . . ." Her blue eyes showed concern, then changed to unease, and she bent hastily to serve the plates. What did she sense? "You need some food, some tea. The scallops were dug this morning on Fentress." When she looked up again, she was more in control and smiled quietly. Both were blocking, a gentle, polite wall placed between them.

Meatha sat admiring Clytey's healthy good looks, remembering too vividly how she had looked when first they escaped the Kubalese caves, thin and ashen, sick from the long weeks drugged by MadogWerg. She supposed she had looked the same. Now Clytey was rosy and lithe—and fast becoming a young lady. Clytey had been only twelve when they came to Carriol. Now at fourteen she was nearly grown.

"Not grown enough," Clytey said, touching her thoughts delicately. "Not grown enough so Alardded will let me dive."

"I didn't know you wanted to."

"I do. Oh, I do, Meatha. He won't let me go even to the bay of Vexin; he says I'm too young and frail. He got so angry. I've never seen Alardded so angry. Meatha, I'm not frail at all. You've seen me work the fields!"

Meatha stared at her. "That's not like Alardded."

"What could the real reason be? I couldn't touch his thoughts. I'm as strong as Roth, or nearly. I'm as strong as Nicoli, even if she does train the horses. What is it about *me?* Oh—I'm sorry. I'm rattling on and you're ill. I—"

"I'm all right, it's . . . I don't understand, either, why he won't let you. Maybe I can talk to him, ask. . . ."

Clytey's eyes brightened, then dulled. "It won't do any good, he's like a rock."

MEATHA PUZZLED over Alardded's attitude and knew she would speak to him about Clytey. Something about Alardded's anger alarmed her sharply, though she could not imagine why. She wanted passionately now to know everything about diving, as if Clytey's very distress had unleashed a heated flood of interest in every detail, in Alardded's every purpose and intention.

She yearned to talk with Alardded, yet found no opportunity before he left for the bay of Vexin, stood watching from the tower early one morning as he and Roth and Nicoli rode out, leading a dozen trained young horses and followed by Hux's wagon. The well-trained horses led easily. It would be a different matter when the band returned leading young, untrained colts to be broken to the ways of saddle and sword and sectbow. Why was Alardded not taking Clytey, when she wanted so much to go? Meatha would have no chance, now, to ask until he returned in five days time.

It was midafternoon of the fifth day when she knew that Alardded's party was returning home. On impulse, she saddled a horse and rode out to meet them, came upon them just at the mouth of the river Somat Cul where it emptied between marshy banks into the sea. They had stopped to mend a broken harness; and while Hux repaired the leather lines, Alardded and Nicoli and young Roth waded knee-deep in the surf, their trousers rolled up like children, laughing. The diving had gone well; they were in high spirits and anxious to be off to Pelli soon for the real dive, filled with eagerness to seek out the drowned runestone at last. She watched the three, concealing her own covetous interest in the drowned stone. They sensed nothing of her thoughts, grinned and waved at her and beckoned her to join them. Nicoli, with her legs bare and her short red hair blowing in the wind, looked no older than Roth. All three were sunburned, Roth deeply burned across his freckled nose.

A dozen young horses were tethered around the marsh on ground stakes, grazing the lush grass. Hux's two older cart horses stood tied on long lines to the back of the wagon, grazing too. Meatha looked with interest at the diving suit hanging to dry on the side of the wagon. It was like a big fat body, for the leather had been stuffed with cloth to keep the wax from cracking—a headless body, for the monster metal head was hanging alongside.

She wanted Alardded to tell her about the diving; but when he began to show her the journey, it was not the diving he brought in vision, but the three new waterwheels along the Somat Cul, the new grain huts nearby, the weaving sheds, the new breeding stock on the farms. Nothing at all of the diving. When they had saddled up once more, she rode alone with Alardded behind the wagon, for Nicoli and Roth had their hands full leading the strings of colts, tied head and tail to one another. At last she clenched her fist on the reins, took a deep breath, and looked across at Alardded. "Did the diving go well?"

"Oh yes, very well." No vision, no sense of what it had been like. His mind as closed as a clamshell.

"Alardded?"

He looked at her, his mind wary. Fear touched her for no reason, and she blocked with all her power, steeled herself to speak. "You did not take Clytey. Why not? She wanted badly to go. To dive with you. She—she is the same size as Nicoli or Roth. The suit would fit her, she—"

Alardded's dark eyes flashed with warning. "Do not ask me, Meatha. I do not wish to discuss that."

"But—" She plunged on despite his annoyance, "Why can't you let her dive? What—?"

"Whether Clytey dives is not your affair. I do not like your speaking of it. This is my business, Meatha, and mine alone."

She had never seen him like this, never seen him so unreasonable. His anger was like a tide. The sense of his mind was utterly closed. He gave her a stormy look, turned his horse and rode away from her. She stared after him, dismayed and afraid. The fear that touched her spread; and a suspicion began to chill her. She tried to call after him and could not.

At last she kicked her horse into a gallop, caught up with him, and forced herself to speak, blurting it out before she could lose her nerve. "Would you let *me* dive, Alardded?"

He did not speak. His mind was like thunder.

"Would you let *me* dive?" She stared at him, willing him to speak.

"I will not let Clytey dive. I will not let you dive. I do not wish to speak of it. The diving is my business, not yours. You are behaving like an insolent child."

"Oh," she said in a small voice, "Oh, but this is my business." For now she knew that she had every right to an answer; and the knowledge terrified her. She tried to breech his shielding, pushing her power at him until his dark eyes turned on her flashing, the muscles of his jaw working as if he bit on steel.

"You take liberties, Meatha. You show the grossest discourtesy to try to breech my mind so! I am the master Seer!" He had never talked down to her before. Her face went hot —but beyond her shame, her uneasy suspicion would not let her turn away. She faced him boldly, her face flaming. "Would you. . . ." Her voice came out like a croak. "Would you let Shoppa dive? Would you let Tocca, if he were old enough? Would you let—any one of us who was drugged in the Kubalese caves?"

Alardded's silence was so complete it was as if they paused in the eye of a storm. Not a breath of air moved between them. He looked suddenly older. His eyes were filled with pain. He gave her one long look, then turned his horse away from her and did not speak nor answer her in his mind.

She sat her horse woodenly, her mind awash with the truth—with the horror of the Kubalese caves, as raw as if it had been yesterday, the feel of the cold stone where she had lain wanting only the drug, more of the drug, the cold terror when the drug was withheld from her, the sense of suffocation, of being crushed by cave walls as if they closed in on her, the terrible panic as she withdrew from the drug, wanting to lash out at the walls and run blindly, her terror of being crushed inside the cave, unable to bear the dark confinement of the cave.

Unable to stand the confinement of the cave. Driven to terror and to madness by confinement.

This was what Alardded knew. That the effects of the drug were not gone. That, given the right circumstances, panic would return. To Clytey; to herself. Given the dark, confining diving suit, given the confinement deep beneath the sea, a victim of the MadogWerg might go mad.

It was with them still, the effects of the drug, would always be with them, unseen and crippling.

She turned her horse away from the others and rode back to the tower alone.

From the Journal of Skeelie of Carriol:

I must try to write of that earlier time before Ram died, before ever we lived as husband and wife. Perhaps if I write of our lives together, I can ease the pain of remembering. And perhaps not, perhaps the pain will only be worse. But I know that I must try.

We came away from that first visit to the city of cones across the unknown mountains carrying Telien. She was so pale, so very close to death. The spirit that had possessed her, the wraith that Ram had driven out, had left little more than a shell, only a small spark of life. We nursed her as best we could, but by morning Telien was dead.

We buried her on an unknown mountainside in the unknown lands. Ram turned from the grave of his lost love in silence, and we headed south at once, where the known countries must lie. Ram walked as if he were alone, wrapped in darkness. But he looked up when we heard the high keening wolf cry on the mountain, and his eyes darkened with a bitter triumph, for we knew then that Torc had destroyed the wraith that had possessed Telien. Too late—too late destroyed. Soon the bitch wolf joined us, filled with her dark vindication.

Our way was slow. We met jagged walls of stone and gashes in the land far too wide and deep to cross. We retraced our steps many times. When at last we found a way over the mountains, we were heading north away from the known countries of Ere. Ram grew impatient then, for which I was grateful, for his armor of mourning seemed less severe. Soon he began to think once more of the four shards of the runestone he carried—and of the shards still to be sought. Slowly and with pain he began to mend from Telien's death, as much as ever he could mend.

We meant to find our way south, back to our own lands, but now Ram seemed pulled northward. We traveled among creatures and plants new and strange to us. Soon we were in high, jagged country, and cold, for a glacier rose to our left beyond a black cliff. It was here we were attacked by huge winged lizards with teeth like knives. We took shelter in an abandoned dwelling place, little more than a few bed-holes carved into the cliff, with narrow steps from one hole to the next, and the bones of game animals littering the floors. But the holes were deep enough so the flying lizards could not reach into them, though they forced clawed talons in, incredibly ugly beasts with wrinkled scaly hides and breath that stunk of decay. The creatures gave away at last, either from boredom or discouragement, and we went on still hoping to find a way south. But the cliff was a sheer wall on our left and rose even taller ahead of us. Soon we came to a deep chasm. We could hardly see the other side, and it stretched so far to our right that it ended in haze against distant peaks. Deep down we could see red molten rivers. The place excited Ram, but the wolves paced restlessly along its lip. Fawdref was as cross and edgy as I have ever seen him, all dark, fierce killer with blazing eyes. Even Torc was upset with the sense of the place, and moved as if she were stalking, head down, watching the abyss. Ram stood at the edge staring down to the fires that burned far below, and I felt his intention chill me long before he spoke. "I must go there, Skeelie. I must go down into that pit."

I was sick with fear for him, but I could say nothing. He must follow his own way.

We were eight years in that valley, living on wild plants and rock hare and deer. Ram studied the abyss and traveled again and again down into it, convinced that somewhere below, among the fires, lay a shard of the runestone of Eresu. He could feel its presence there, touching him. I knew he would never leave that place without it—and he did not leave it, not in body.

Our son was born in that valley.

We found a shelter of boulders that first day, to make a beginning dwelling, and piled stones to enlarge it. I thatched the roof to cover the cracks between the boulders, and Ram went to hunt

*with the wolves. As easily as that we established a home. Though it
was a long time more before we lived as husband and wife. The delay
was not my doing. When Ram healed at last from the worst of his
mourning, I was able to ease his pain somewhat, to give him of
warmth and gentleness, someone to cling to. I hid my joy from him.
I was afraid to let him know how much I cared.*

*From the entrance to our rock home, gazing southwest, we
could see in the far distance beyond the cliff and beyond the white
apron of the glacier, a peak rising so high and alone that Ram felt
sure it was Tala-charen. He could feel a power from that peak that
seemed to reach toward our desolate valley, a power he felt was
linked to the runestone. He was more and more certain that a shard
of the runestone lay down in the burning chasm, and sometimes he
felt a presence down there, too, as if a living thing were watching
us. I could not speak my fears to him, nor would I turn him aside. I
knew I might see him die, but I would not hinder what he must
surely do. We went again and again into the pit. It was a place of
mystery, of shifting smoke, the changing lava flows and the falling
stones tearing away the land so our way was never the same. We
saw fire ogres there with flame playing across their thick, wrinkled
hides, ogres only the heaviest arrows could kill. And something
larger and infinitely more evil lay in that abyss, a creature formed
perhaps from the heart of the abyss itself. Something that watched us
at first only half-alive, that followed the sense of our movements,
followed the sense of power from the runestones Ram carried with
ever growing interest; as if it were slowly acquiring life, slowly
becoming more powerful.*

*Could the stone that lay in that abyss have nurtured such a
creature? Could a shard of the runestone, if it lay long enough
immersed in that evil place, have bred evil? Bred a creature that, on
sensing Ram's four runestones, quickened to life further and thirsted
for ultimate power? Or was there another explanation? And how
did the runestone get into the abyss? And when?*

*The creature moved unseen, eventually tracking us and tracked
by us. Over the years its power became stronger and the sense of its*

size seemed to increase. And then at last the sense of its name came to us. It called itself Dracvadrig. We sensed that sometimes it was like a man, sometimes like a great worm. And it had about it the essence of death. Had it risen from death or near death? Was it a creature like the wraith, perhaps? The wraith had once been a man, given over to the drug MadogWerg and to the evils that grew from it. Was this thing in the pit the same, a man unable to die, growing after his body's death into another form? Had it lain in the pit long after its death, its moldering body couched around the runestone before life came seeping back sufficiently for it to rise and watch us, and to grow slowly into the monsterous dragon that we saw at last? I do not know. I only know that it was Dracvadrig who killed Ram.

I did not go with Ram into the pit that day, nor had for some days, for Lobon was ill with fever. Torc and Rhymannie were excellent nurses, but I could not leave Lobon when he was so sick. Ram gave into my hands the four runestones so that I could help him with their power, and I stood watching as the twelve wolves descended with him into the abyss. I had no premonition that Dracvadrig would rise that day to show itself, that it would at last challenge Ram. I sent my power with them, and later I stood reaching with all my force into the battle Ram waged against the creature. Even Lobon's young, untrained power came strong then, to defend Ram, our powers focused through the runestones in a battle soon turned desperate, then terrifying, the wolves leaping and tearing at the dragon as it flailed and twisted in battle, its screams of fury echoing across the pit and between the mountains. And the power of the stone it possessed struck against Ram and against the stones I wielded with a force that made me reel with its intensity. I used every power, every force I knew, felt Ram's furious, angry battle, his powers linked with mine against the creature as if we stood side by side. Lobon, his face flushed with the fever, had come to stand beside me, his power raging against the dragon, more power in that moment than I had thought any child could contain.

But our powers were not enough. Ram's strength was not

enough, nor the wolves' fierce and continued attacks. Perhaps other forces fought beside the dragon, forces of the dark. I felt that this was so, and wondered if they had watched us longer than we ever knew.

Ram was wounded. He lay dying. He was dead before I reached him. Climbing and running down into the pit, I could only think over and over, If only I had been with him battling with sword as well as with the stones.

But I cannot dwell on that. It likely would have made no difference. Yet I do dwell, am sick with it even yet. I wake sometimes seeing him die, and cry out into the night before I can stop myself.

I lashed together a sapling drag to bring Ram's body out. Five wolves stood guard over him. Seven wolves lay dead. Fawdref lay dead, his dark coat smeared with blood, his body torn by the dragon's claws. Torc and Rhymannie were badly hurt. They limped out slowly, not able even to keep pace with the drag. As I turned away from the scene of battle after my first climb, I saw the wounded dragon creeping toward me. I spun and raised my bow, but the creature was hurt and clawed at the cliff then slipped and fell deeper into the pit. Suddenly it stayed its fall, with leathery wings raised, and beat its way clumsily skyward, twisting as if at any minute it would fall again. It must have been near to death at that moment, not to have come after the stones I held close inside my tunic, yet it flew up out of the pit, scrambling and clawing at the stone walls, and disappeared over the farther lip of the abyss where lay the unknown lands. Whether it returned to the abyss or not, I do not know. But every creature returns to its nest.

We buried Ram and Fawdref and the six young, strapping wolves who died with them in the stone room that had been our first home, made a cairn of that place and covered the entrance with rocks. Lobon worked in stoic silence, ignoring his fever, carrying rocks to secure his father's grave. Five days later, when Lobon was well and the bitch wolves had begun to heal, I set fire to the larger, sapling hut that Ram and I had built together and burned it to the ground. Then we went away to the east, where lay the city of cones,

*Lobon and I and five wolves, silent in our mourning; Lobon so
broken by Ram's death that it was many months before he could shed
a tear.*

*We remained among the people of the city of cones until the
pain of Ramad's death began to heal for me. Lobon, even at six years
old, was filled with such cold fury that I felt it would never abate.*

*Then, as I mourned in the city of cones, Canoldir spoke to me
across Time. He spoke again and again, this man who lived outside
of Time, and at last he helped me to see life around me once more,
and I was glad for his caring.*

*We came to Canoldir at last, after nearly two years, came in
an instant of Time, Lobon and I and the wolves, an instant of
dizziness and shock, moving across Time and outside of Time to
stand suddenly in Canoldir's villa, where I had stood only once before
—beside Ram.*

*Canoldir is gentle with me. He is helping me to heal as much as
ever I will be healed, until I know Ram again in some life yet to
come to us.*

Excerpt from pages written some time later in Skeelie's
life with Canoldir:

*And even now, though I dwell outside of Time and have touched
knowledge that was before closed to me, I do not know what
Dracvadrig is. Canoldir thinks he was once a man, that he stood in
Tala-charen at the moment of the splitting and received a shard of
the runestone; that he let the darkness lure him with that stone until
he was drawn into the evil caverns of Urdd; that he grew there in
evil until at last he took the dragon form in a dull, half-somnolent
life. And then, awakened by the powers of Ramad's stones, came
again fully alive, this time in a rising, lusting evil. Surely there was
a strength beyond the power of one shard of the runestone in that
abyss when Dracvadrig killed Ramad; it was as if the powers of dark
dwelt with him, and strengthened him.*

But even Canoldir's knowledge of this is limited, for something new touches us in this place outside of Time. Canoldir can no longer move so freely, at will, through Time. No longer See into all times freely to solve such mysteries. Is this place, our home, beginning to move back into the river of Time? Canoldir has begun to show small signs of aging, too—which only make him the handsomer. Something is happening to Ere even here, powers drawing in and shifting, as do the forces of the mountains themselves, power driving against power until surely something must give, in fury and in violence.

Will the fabric of Ere's powers heave and twist as do the mountains? Is what we are experiencing now a part of this, is Lobon's search for Dracvadrig a part of this, is the pitting of stone against stone a part?

And what part did Ram's life play in focusing such powers—or in staying them, in quelling them so to delay some possible holocaust?

What if Ramad had never been born, and the runestone never split?

Oh, but Ram was born; Ere would not have been complete without him. I loved him, and I can never cease to mourn him in my heart and in my soul, and in the way I touch life now; though I never can touch life very gently, I never could. Canoldir chides me, and laughs at me for that, just as Ramad did.

Part Two

Heritage of the Dark

Chapter
Five

SKEELIE PACED, restless as a river cat. Her dark hair, knotted crookedly, caught the firelight. Canoldir watched her from where he sprawled on hide-covered cushions in the shadows beyond the hearth. He was concerned for her but smiling, too, at the force of her anger. She stared back at him, tense and irritable. "Lobon moves there now, into the abyss, just as Ramad did. It is nothing to be amused about. How can you —it means nothing to you! Nothing!" Though she knew that was not so.

"It means, my love, more than you know. But give the lad room, give him time. Give him room to breathe, room to make mistakes and recover from them."

"He's had all his life to make mistakes. This is not the time. If he makes a mistake there—I can feel the evil of Drac-vadrig like a stench. And, Canoldir, I think there are others there, I sense other presences. Lobon does not know what awaits him. He does not go there as Ramad did, with a purpose larger than himself. He goes with personal anger, personal hatred. He does not do justice to what Ram was, he—"

"Then your anger is not for Lobon's safety, my love, nor for the safety of the stones—but at Lobon's disrespect for Ramad!"

"It is his ignorance! There is danger in his willful ignorance!" She stared at Canoldir's reclining shape, wished he would come out of the shadows and stop lounging like a bear. His dark hair and beard blended with the hair on the coarse hides, his eyes, from the shadows, saw too much, his mind Saw too much. She turned away from him toward the fire's blaze and rested her head against the high mantel. When she looked back at him at last, it was with more conviction. "I feel something else, too. I feel a force moving out from Tala-charen, the force that Ram felt. What is that power? It touches the abyss. It seems to reach toward Carriol, too, toward that shard of the runestone. It is a power that belongs to the stones, Canoldir, that comes from the mountain where the whole runestone once lay."

Canoldir sat up. His eyes never left her. "I think it is in truth a power born of the mountain and of the forces that placed the stone there. A power that is only a part of the great forces that made and nurture Ere—forces neither good nor bad, Skeelie. But forces that can feed on the powers of either." He paused, pulled on his beard, deep in thought. "The pow-ers of the earth can be wed to either darkness or light. The master of Urdd would wed himself to the earth's powers and bring them ultimately into the realm of the dark, and his very commitment to the dark gives him strength."

She stared back at him. "And Lobon has not wedded himself to any power but his own." She sighed, began to pace again. "Lobon faces the master of Urdd with too little belief, too little commitment to the stones and their destiny. Drac-vadrig means to destroy him, and he has not the strength even that Ram had. Is he blind? Doesn't he see? Did Ram die only that Lobon could gratify his own mindless need for revenge and lose his life—and lose the runestones forever? Give over Ere forever to evil?"

Canoldir rose and came to her. He held her until at last her fears drew back; though the darkness remained across their minds like a sickness as the forces of dark knit and swelled.

THE BLACK CLIFF stood in shadow, a last ray of sun touching along its top edge, the abyss below nearly dark except for the red glow of its fires. Within the cliff in the small cave room, Kish stood, sensing out across Ere as delicately as a snake senses. For she, too, felt forces amassing, felt dark spirits stirring in Ere's depths, waking, rising out of rocky graves. Kish smiled, coldly and eagerly.

As she watched the abyss below, the scenes of the last days came to her, Dracvadrig leading the young Seer ever deeper into the abyss, teasing him ever more sharply, until now the son of Ramad had been driven into a shallow cave where he stood panting and so angry he was hardly master of himself; hardly master of even his limited skills, in his fury. And Dracvadrig waited beyond a stone shelf, blocking his presence, ready to strike again.

LOBON LEANED against the cave wall trying to stop the excessive bleeding from a long wound down his arm. The wolves prowled the cliffs below, but Dracvadrig was gone from the abyss, Lobon could feel its emptiness.

Now he and the wolves were no longer the hunters, now Dracvadrig hunted them, stalked them with a silent stealth that neither Lobon's powers nor the powers of the wolves— or of the stones themselves—had been able to avert. He did not understand the increasing power of the firemaster. In a series of quick skirmishes, the dragon had attacked and slashed, then flown off, blocking and twisting their senses, easing them into defense, playing with them over and over until they were able to follow only for short distances, battle, then flee deeper into the abyss. They would be struck from behind to turn facing only the empty pit. He knew his anger destroyed his judgement, he knew the wolves were cross and edgy. He fought the knowledge of defeat with added fury. Great Urdd, he was tired, aching tired, his leathers soaked with sweat and stinking. Always too hot, always fighting the ever-present black gnats that stung and made him itch beyond bearing. He thought longingly of cold water, dreamed of sinking deep into a cool river, of drinking his fill of cool water.

He knew his intent to kill Dracvadrig had deteriorated into the dream of an incompetent child. He was shamed at his own loss of control and unable to do anything to change the desperate debilitating anger that drove him on so uselessly. Certainly he would not turn back. He would follow Dracvadrig to the very center of Ere if he must. His hatred was a tide pummeling him, and he would not give in ever.

Shorren came up the cliff to him and pressed close, nudging his hand. *You must sleep, Lobon. You must eat the rest of the roasted snake, drink and sleep. We will take watch in turns.*

BEHIND THEM, the dragon smiled and considered its prey, as sporting in its contemplation of Lobon as a hunting cat is sporting with soft furry creatures to behead. Neither Lobon nor the wolves sensed it. Its power in the stone had grown strong and facile as other dark powers rose across Ere to buoy it—no powers of the Seers of light had so joined forces to create a tide of strength as had the forces of dark. Even the Seers of Carriol were not sufficiently joined and aggressive. Some, at least the girl, were easily led and turned aside, so easily turned to the dark.

MEATHA'S SUDDEN VISION came so strong she was unaware of having stopped on the stone stairs. A vision of fear struck her so sharply she cried out a silent warning and didn't know to whom she cried. She blocked at once from the people moving past her up toward the citadel. She was unaware of the sea light glancing through a portal, did not notice people pause to look at her. Fear, crushing fear from someone filled her; then she was aware of Lobon, saw his angry scowl, his tousled red hair, her vision of the abyss so real she might have been standing beside him.

How intense he was, his dark eyes fierce as an animal's, the tangle of his red hair wild as windborne fire. He unnerved her, attracted her, and she was terrified for him. She felt his willful rebelliousness—and she knew his spirit intimately in that moment, a spirit raw, wanting, and untamed. Knew the danger that waited so close, unseen. And, in spite of his danger and his vulnerability, she felt the power that dwelt about him, and she puzzled at it. And then suddenly she knew what it was, and she stood wide-eyed, not believing. Then having to believe: this Seer carried runestones hidden beneath his bloody tunic. Four shards of the runestone of Eresu.

And she knew with a sudden wildness matching his own, with a rising sense of her own power, that she must tame this man; and that she must have the stones. That to take the runestone that hung in the citadel alone was not enough. She saw her mission suddenly as whole and complete: Everything was linked, all the stones were linked: she must have them all, if ever she were to help Ere. The last hint of her self-doubt fled; she had touched power now, and she would hold to it. She began to plan.

First she must rescue the stone that hung in the citadel. She could never make the council understand that she must take it, that only through carrying it into battle could Kubal be defeated. No one in Carriol was willing to take the stone from its safe place. Once she had that stone then—then she must retrieve the stone that Alardded would surely bring from the sea. And then the stones this young Seer held, deep in the fiery pit. It was all so clear, so essential. As if a pattern of her destiny had been laid down long before she was born: to discover the stone in Burgdeeth and bring it here: then, in Carriol, to learn the skills she would need, and at last to carry the stone and its mates in a final powerful defeat of the dark forces she so hated. She was so engrossed in what she must do that she forgot her fear for Lobon, or that he was in danger, could think only of her role in Ere's salvation.

To rescue the stone in citadel, she must have the mare. She could not escape without a winged one to carry her. Michennan must come, in spite of her reluctance. She pressed her back against the cold stone of the stair well and brought the vision of Michennann around her sharply until she felt as if she herself stood in the far green field where Michennann grazed.

MICHENNANN STOOD with dripping muzzle. She had been feeding on lilies in the water meadow. Now she looked southeast toward Carriol, held within her the sweep of Meatha's whispering mind, urgent and irritating, then laid back her ears and shook her head, not liking the demanding summons.

She was a beautiful mare, the color of deep storm. Across one shoulder blazed a streak of white that ended beneath her dark mane. Her eyes were dark, the lashes silver against endless depths of darkness, her wings when she lifted them against the morning sky were silver, though they shadowed down to night where the feathers overlapped. She acknowledged Meatha's presence with annoyance, examined deeply Meatha's purpose; bowed her neck and tucked her head down in hard defiance. The girl's quest had a darkness to it, a darkness Michennann wanted no part of, though she and Meatha were old friends. Friendship was one thing, this stealthy darkness quite another. What had changed Meatha? Or did she not see the dark that touched her?

Meatha scowled at the mare's resistance. What was wrong with Michennann? She pressed harder still, then too late she realized her error, for the mare had drawn away from her completely and closed her mind with a stubborn will, her tail switching with anger.

Meatha drew back too, and waited. She would not be put off. When the mare had calmed somewhat, she touched her mind more gently, carefully began to soothe Michennann, to calm her. Slowly she gentled and quieted her own driving force and washed away the tension, softened the tension between them until at last their minds could link in a smoother flow. She soothed the mare and soothed her, until after some moments Michennann relaxed satisfactorily; her ears went forward, she lifted one forefoot wet from the marsh meadow and gazed without fury into the southeastern sky.

Michennann held in suspension the last of her unease, the shadow of her reluctance. She let lie at bay the darkness that had now submerged itself beneath Meatha's gentleness —but she would not forget it. She felt the danger in what Meatha was about, her fear unformed and nebulous but very real.

But she would follow Meatha. For the sake of something she could not put shape to, she knew she would follow her.

She turned to stare at the band of winged ones who stood silently at the other end of the meadow and spoke to them. They moved uneasily, but they did not reply. Michennann pushed back the unease, like rain-blindness, that shadowed her thoughts. She bowed her neck, and broke suddenly from a standstill into a gallop. She was skyborne in three strides, her neck stretched out, her dark nose cutting the wind.

IN VISION, Meatha Saw the mare lift skyward, and she turned away with satisfaction; though still she held a tight, gentle snare of power around Michennann, drawing her toward Carriol. She was aware once again of folk passing her on the stone stair. She let her blocking ease for a moment as her tension eased, turned to follow them, sharpening her blocking again at once.

It would not be easy to sit among others with her secret filling her and yet maintain the constant blocking needed to shut out master Seers. But the urgency of her mission seemed to give her power, and now she felt capable of anything.

Michennann would graze out on Fentress unnoticed until they could depart—until Alardded had departed for Pelli.

Her timing must be perfect. Not too soon, not until Alardded was just on the verge of bringing up the drowned runestone. Too soon, and she could be discovered, Alardded alerted. She joined the meeting at last with reluctance, sat down near the entry, and looked over the heads of those in front to where the five master Seers sat circling the stone table. The runestone moved slightly in the sea breeze. She dared not look directly at it for fear her expression would give her away. Alardded and Bernaden had left a space between them, and a man stood respectfully behind the stone bench there, facing the five council Seers with obvious awe. A tall, pale man with a curiously small head and thin shoulders, larger in the trunk and hips, heavy legged—rather like a bag of grain with most of the grain run to the bottom. He was the reason for the meeting: a man brought to Carriol unexpectedly, a prisoner rescued from Kubal. He came from out a land they had thought uninhabited, from the unknown lands inside the Ring of Fire. His voice was loud for such a weak-looking person. He answered Alardded's questions simply, artlessly.

The city he had come from was as remarkable as he, a city of stone cones naturally formed, perhaps by the volcanoes, and the cones hollowed out by patient carving to make dwellings. Here he had lived all his life. His name was Fithern. He answered their questions carefully, but glanced again and again at the suspended runestone, could not keep his eyes from it, and at last Alardded stopped the questions and allowed Fithern to speak as he would. He was silent for a long while, then he said hesitantly but with excitement.

"*She* carried such stones as that! *She* carried two of them, and a handful of golden ones, too, stones like stars on fire." There was utter silence in the citadel. No Seer moved.

"And who was *she?*" Bernaden said softly. Her chestnut hair and high coloring were caught by the sea light. Her gentle eyes tried to warm the stranger.

"The lady of the wolves, Seer," he said at last. "The lady

who traveled with wolves by her side, who came to our city the first time with the prince of wolves himself." Fithern sighed."But when she came to the city of cones the second time, with her child, then the prince of the wolves was not with her. Then the prince of the wolves was dead." There was a great sadness in his voice, as if he mourned a wonderful and inexplicable glory. Still no Seer stirred.

"What prince of wolves?" Alardded asked softly. "What lady? Of what time do you speak, Fithern? Of your own time? Did you see such people?"

"Oh yes, in my time, Seer. Though I was very young. The lord and lady of the wolves released our people from a possession, where men moved mindlessly. From possession by a goddess that the lady of the wolves called Wraith— though sometimes she spoke of the creature as Telien. The lady and the prince of the wolves took the goddess away with them and drove its spirit out. They carried the green stones; and when the lady returned, she had them still—four stones, she said, though one was the golden starfires, and one was hidden inside a strange bell that she used to hold when she held the stones, and that would make the wolves cry out. She told us a green stone was inside.

Alardded sat silent. Surely this man spoke of Ramad, but in their own time? How was that possible? And who was the woman? Then one fact startled them all, the knowledge of it flying among them: they could not read Fithern's thoughts.

Was that, then, why they had not known of the city of cones, never guessed that these people existed? Surely so.

Tra. Hoppa had come to sit among the Seers, drawn to this man. Her voice was quick and eager, her eyes bright. "How do you know that when the lady of the wolves returned without . . . returned alone, that the lord of the wolves was dead?"

"She mourned for him. She wept in her dwelling alone. She told my people he was dead."

"And what happened to her?" Tra. Hoppa whispered.

"One day she went away with the wolves and her child and no one saw them go. Everything was left behind, hides, bedding, extra clothes, the pieces of pale parchment she liked to write upon."

"Parchment, Fithern? And where is it now?" Tra. Hoppa's voice rose, could hardly contain her excitement. "And what does the parchment tell?"

"It lies in her dwelling just as she left it, lady, ten years gone. But I don't know what it tells. None of us can read writing."

He had fled the city of cones when a wandering band of Kubalese had come upon it and murdered many. He had been taken captive by another such band somewhere in the Urobb hills. "They held me for a while in the camp of the leader, Kearb-Mattus," he said. "I know who *he* is. And I know the Seer RilkenDal. I learned much from the other captives. I saw Kearb-Mattus and RilkenDal myself once, walking among the captive horses. The Seer RilkenDal was tall and dark and twisted in his walk, and he was choosing horses and causing a strangeness to come over them so they followed him unfettered like dogs."

Meatha shuddered and huddled into herself. The darkness was moving in around them, moving on Carriol ever more powerfully, dark forces closing them in, forces that *must* be destroyed.

Only the runestone, the whole runestone, could ever defeat such darkness.

She looked up at the jade at last, so rich a green, suspended alone. It turned in the breeze, catching the sea light. The stone would mark her way. The stone would save Ere, and she would be its servant, to carry it.

It was then she Saw Lobon in sharp vision, Saw that he slept; Saw the dragon slipping close to him and felt his peril sharply. Hardly aware of the Seers around her, blocking without thinking, she brought power in the stone, fierce and sudden—so tense, so lost in vision was she that she was unaware of anything around her as she drove her forces against the advancing dragon. Her blocking was a mindless power born of her lifelong need. The creature she challenged was stalking Lobon like a cat stalking a shrew. It must not kill this Seer. It must not have the stones, she knew no other emotion but this.

Chapter
Six

EVEN IN HIS SLEEP Lobon was pursued. His dreams never let him free. In dreams he stalked the dragon and turned to find it ready to spring; and then in his dreams the earth trembled, and he thought that, too, was Dracvadrig's spell.

But the earth did stir. The wakeful wolves felt it, five quick shocks. They leaped to the mouth of the cave and stood watching the abyss. Pebbles rolled down from above. A lizard slithered to gain purchase on the shelf where it had fallen, and Crieba snatched it up. The ground shook under their feet. Behind them, Lobon rolled over in his sleep, but he did not wake. Shorren began to move out along the cliff, then she drew back snarling as another, harsher shock caught them. A wind hit them suddenly, and Dracvadrig was above them sweeping down out of nowhere. How long had the dragon been watching and waiting there? He twisted in midair before the cave and began to coil around boulders, towering over the opening, dwarfing the abyss. Lobon came awake then, as the dragon struck at the wolves; they leaped at its scaly throat; Lobon snatched up his sword and lunged, slashed across its neck. It lurched away screaming with anger, left blood at their feet. Its roar joined with the roar of the earth as the abyss rocked and shuddered. The dragon twisted on the wind and dove again, its great head seeking Lobon, flame gushing between yellowed teeth; he dodged, and it caught him by the shoulder, lifted him—and he felt another power with him fiercely driving at the dragon as it shook him. Dizzy, hurting, he found his knife. The dragon reared on the narrow shelf, he felt the earth beneath it heave, heard the shelf crack beneath the dragon's weight, felt the creature falling, as it still gripped him between its jaws. He slashed, was grazed by a rock, fell with the dragon in the shower of stones. He felt the other power with him swelling, battling. Skeelie? No, not Skeelie. He caught a glimpse of the girl's face, of the swinging rune-stone. He felt the force of power she poured into that stone for him.

He landed across the dragon's coils beside its gaping jaw, lay facing one huge watchful eye. He was sick with pain and knew that in a moment Dracvadrig would reach, open that great jaw and destroy him. Driven by urgency, he leaped and plunged the sword deep into the eye. A cry of rage shattered around him. Blood spurted from the eye. The dragon twisted away, flailing and whipping across the chasm. Then suddenly it rose upward, screaming, its wings dragging its body up toward the rim.

It disappeared, half flying, half flailing, over the lip of the abyss.

The earth stilled. Lobon let out his breath, felt his reprieve, was sharply aware of the one instant, the one lucky blow. Was Dracvadrig dying? Elated, he began to climb up toward the mouth of the cave. Pain tore through his shoulder and arm. The wolves pushed around him. He leaned on Feldyn, forgetting elation then, in pain, and let the wolf pull him upward.

ABOVE THE ABYSS in the black cliff, a pale figure moved to the portal. She watched Dracvadrig approaching in slow awkward flight as if at any minute he would fall back to the rocks below. She saw without emotion the dragon's face covered with blood and the ruined eye.

At last she heard him come into the cave entrance behind her. He was losing control, beginning to change into the form of a man. She watched the change intently, until at last he lay sprawled across the stone bench, his lined face gray with pain, the gouged eye running blood.

She tended him coldly, mopping away the blood. She gave him a small portion of eppenroot for the pain.

"Haven't you got MadogWerg! This is putrid stuff!"

"No, Drac. None." Then, with disgust, "Your eye will not mend. You must use your Seeing senses to replace it."

He stared at her in fury. His thin lined face was distorted with pain—and then as the drug took effect, distorted with its hold on him. "You needn't be so pleased."

"*You* let it happen! You play with your quarry too much. Why didn't you—"

"Why didn't I what? Kill him and take the stones? Where would our plan be then?"

"You could have taken them without killing him. You didn't have to get yourself made half useless!"

He did not answer her. Whatever hatred flared between them at the moment, both knew they needed Lobon. Presently he said, "The Seer will be in the cells soon. He is already nearly on top of the gates."

"How can you be sure he will keep on toward the cells?"

"I laid a false sense of my presence. Do you think me an imbecile?"

"All right, Drac. All right."

"Where is RilkenDal?"

"Gone. To fight beside Kearb-Mattus. Gone to deliver mounts from the cells." She spat against the wall. "His pets! Hateful animals. All that screaming. The disgusting whimpers of brute creatures."

"They are useful, my dear. RilkenDal's troops cannot move across Ere on dragon wings as you are fortunate enough to do."

"Nasty beasts all the same. Talking like men, pretending to the wisdom of Seers—such as it is. He would be better off with flying lizards. They are more natural."

"And stubborn and stupid and bad-tempered." He eased back on the stone bench. "The countries are beginning to panic, Kish. RilkenDal must move ahead now. Now is the time to attack."

Kish smiled coldly. "Soon all of Ere will be ours."

"It is not ours yet," he said testily. "We must watch the girl. Make sure she is successful. I cannot lose my hold on her. Ah, Kish, once we possess the two runestones she will bring us, and the four the boy carries. . . ." He shook the stone in the golden casket that dangled at his waist. "Seven stones, Kish. Seven shards of the runestone."

"You don't have his four yet."

"I have them. I simply let him carry them. It makes the chase more exciting." He did not mention his ruined eye. He was close to euphoria with the drug, dulled and rested and inane. "Think, Kish, when the stone is joined . . . ." She smiled and nodded and stared at him appraisingly.

"With the power of all the stones . . . ." He laughed drunkenly. "Oh I will have the nine stones, and soon. And then the son of Ramad will be useful!" His long face warped into an evil smile, twisted with the drug and maimed into a mask of horror by the gory eye.

"Will you have them, Drac?" she said cruelly. "You let him defeat you just now. The whelp and the powers that joined him defeated you. Are you too drugged to remember that the *girl* helped him!" She rose and began to pace. "You had best keep better control, Drac. You had best move that girl quickly! And that band of Seers moving among my cults —I have groomed those cults too carefully to allow. . . ."

His laugh became a giggle. He lounged drunkenly on the bench, as if he had forgotten the injured eye, perhaps the socket was as numb now as if no eye had ever existed. "The cults will not dare turn from you, my dear. Though perhaps you are right, perhaps it is time you appeared among them. Perhaps their goddess has been absent too long. I should like to play with some foe besides that puny young Seer for a change. He will follow the trail I laid. The ogres will see to his capture." He made an effort to rise. "Shall we journey to the battles, my dear? Witness the fun, speak to your multitudes? Ah, then I will be close to the young woman as she brings the stones out of Pelli."

Kish scowled. "Can you change back to dragon and hold that form with the drug on you? I don't want. . . . Are you in condition to carry us?"

He felt the neck wound with long exploring fingers, did not touch his eye, moved restlessly, stared at her glassily for some moments with the one good eye. He was trying to change. After some moments, when he remained in the form of a man, he rose unsteadily, took the runestone from its casket, spoke to it, trying to draw power from it.

Nothing happened, he was impotent with the effects of the drug, remained humiliatingly trapped in the human body. Kish watched him with disgust.

At last she drew close to him, scowling at his weakness but unwilling to be deprived of his usefulness. Her voice fell into a soft chant, smooth as honey. "I feel the dark Seers waking, Drac," she crooned. "I have felt all day their voices calling up out of infinite darkness." Her voice flowed as compelling and hypnotizing as the spell of a snake luring its prey. "Dark Seers, Drac, dark Seers waking in darkness, keening to the call of the runestones, their spirits rising to draw together and join us, to join the power of the stones. The spirits of the dead Seers, Drac, the spirits of those in whom the spark has lain as dead—too long idle, they will join us now; they will be one with us now, I feel the power of the Hape, of dark beings beyond the Ring of Fire rising—never dead, never really dead." Her pale hands lifted and caressed him. The firemaster stared at her, bound to her caressing voice. "Now our time is coming, Drac, now our strength gathers, now we will quell the light-struck rule of Carriol." She wet her lips with a pale tongue. "Too long have they held the stone, Drac, too long their cloying light washed that which should couch itself in darkness, too long spoken of *love*, and of *honor*. I feel the dark Seers, Dracvadrig, I feel their spirits waking from times long past, NiMarn who fashioned the wolf bell, NilokEm and his get, HarThass, who failed so miserably to win the soul of Ramad—I feel the dark core of each rising now, I feel powers huge and pulsing, breathing life into those who have slept. Their spirits rise, Drac, they will join us. Feel it, Dracvadrig. Feel them touching you."

Her mesmerization gripped and immersed him, transported him until, at long last his body began to change into the dragon form, his legs to swell and shape into a coil that writhed and swelled, his wrinkled fingers to lengthen into heavy claws, his long nose and sharp chin to elongate further into dragon face. The wounded eye was larger, a dragon's ruined eye, and blood flowed from it anew. His coils filled the cave and pressed Kish back against the stone wall. She caressed the cold dragon flesh with pale hands, stroked the creature's leathery wings that pushed against the roof trying to break free.

All across Ere from dim, deep caverns and dark fissures, the dark listened to Kish and strove and sought out for its kindred spirits, for presences beginning to wake after generations of sleep. These rose as a stench would rise from moldering bodies; and each, waking, joined the next: the spirit of the Hape, the worm gantroed, the ice cat, creatures shunned by animals of light. Now their essences sought to become one, joining with the spirits of dark Seers, joining with the darkness that rode within Kish and within Dracvadrig and RilkenDal, within all who moved in evil across Ere.

Slowly Dracvadrig slid toward the mouth of the cave,

until he filled the opening with swelling coils. Kish slipped onto his back. He slid out and down the cliff's side, then lifted his heavy wings and beat drunkenly skyward, into the heavy wind.

They headed south, Kish's icy hands caressing dragon mane, her thoughts leaping ahead to battles, to the disciplining of her cults, to the destruction of the young Seers who meddled with them. Her anticipation of that destruction was eager and keen.

ZEPHY LOOKED UP from poulticing the chest of a sick child, shivered, and didn't know why. She could bring no vision, but was awash with unease suddenly. She shook back her hair, frowned, all her spirit filled with foreboding; kneeling there by the child, the steaming poultice forgotten, she sought Thorn in her thoughts.

Thorn sensed what she sensed and hid his sudden fear from the men he was drilling; cultists, so slow to learn battle practices.

But now suddenly these men stood confronting him with sharper attention. They seemed wider awake. He stopped his lesson and examined the change in them. Their expressions had become suddenly alert, their minds alert. Some looked no longer docile and obedient, but now looked defiant. And then they began to chant, a harsh whisper that carried across the camp.

"She comes."

"The warrior queen comes."

"The warrior queen speaks to us."

"She moves across the winds to us."

Zephy's thoughts touched his mind, cutting across the chant. *What is it? What's happening?*

I don't—But the chants faded abruptly. The scene before Thorn faded as if a sudden fog engulfed the campground. Another scene, of battle, took its place. They Saw the city of

Zandour, Saw new troops attacking from the sky, dark warriors mounted on horses of Eresu. Winged ones harnessed and bitted and driven with whips—and driven by some strange compelling power that held them more captive than any harness could do. Then the winged ones were dwarfed in the sky by a monster dragon come out of cloud to dive with them down upon Zandour's troops: the earthbound horses screamed and fell under its claws, under blows from the sky, their riders slashed by the swords of skyborne riders.

The dragon swept low over the city licking out flame so the city began to burn, a house here, a barn, wherever its fiery breath caught. And astride the dragon rode a pale, tall woman slashing and killing with a heavy sword. The dragon swept low against the walls of the ruling house of Zandour, once Hermeth's home, and the walls fell as if eggshells had crumbled. On the hillside, the marker of Hermeth's grave was ripped away with one glancing blow, and Hermeth's moldering frail bones ripped out and scattered and trampled into dust. And then, as suddenly as the vision came to Zephy and Thorn, it vanished, for Kish spun a blocking force around Zandour to confuse and terrify the Seers further.

The horror of that destruction, then the sudden absence of any vision, was felt like a shock across Ere; was felt in the far high deserts as a final challenge that started with the scattering of Hermeth's bones. There on the desert a band of wolves paused with raised heads to listen, to watch, their lifted faces stern as they stared away past the brutal sands toward the countries below the rim, toward Zandour, whence the vision came.

They were wolves come long ago to the high desert, come generations before out of Zandour, descendants of those who had not joined Ramad when he was swept away out of Time. They had come to the desert and lived generations here; and now suddenly they harked to the pillage in Zandour, to the world their ancestors had left. They felt the warring with a cold fury; and they felt the darkness rising. They Saw the dragon and his woman attacking Zandour's troops. Their race-memory, and the tales handed down from their sires, knew the kindness in Zandour, knew the gentleness of Hermeth; and they recalled the way in which Hermeth died, possessed by darkness.

They turned as one to look off toward the north's uncharted mountains where the wolf bell dwelt and where the son of Ramad stalked and swore, fettered by his own fury against full use of the stones he carried. And all time and all evils and all forms of goodness came together into a wholeness for them. A pale dog wolf raised his muzzle and howled. A dark brother joined him, and another. A bitch wolf screamed into the hot desert wind. The band's cry sent a chill across the high desert that made rock hares freeze in their tracks and lone miners pull their doors to and bolt them.

And suddenly the band leaped away running hard for the rim and for the lands below it.

A PALE, WHITE-HAIRED CHILD heard their cry like wonderful music and watched them leave the desert. When she turned back toward her small valley at last, she walked swiftly and did not pause until she had curled into her bed beneath the crystal dome and held once more in her small hand the heavy talisman she kept always with her. Now, soon, they would come, a Seer would come searching for the stone. A Seer of light? Or a dark Seer? She could not yet divine which. The dark Seer might kill her, but such a one could not take the stone.

Would the other white-haired ones come now?

She prayed for the salvation of Ere, prayed until at last a vision of the Luff'Eresi came to her like cascading light through the crystal dome, their forms glinting through the heavy crystal panes as if the dome existed not at all, tall iridescent beings seeming half man, half horse, but more wonderful than either, creatures whose great wings shed rainbow light; and she thought of them as gods though they were not; and she spoke to them as she would to gods.

"Will you help them?" she whispered. "Will you help them now?"

We do not know. They must help themselves.

But even with that vague answer she felt eased; and long after they had left her, she lay dreaming contentedly, the heavy green jade clutched tight in her small pale fist.

A FEW REMNANTS of the Zandourian army escaped the dragon and fell back under cover of darkness to restore what was left of their decimated battalions. Scouts slipped away to outlying farms to gather reinforcements, though new soldiers would be very young, for the young were all that was left. New horses would be half-wild colts, or old and stiff. And food was growing short, weapons in short supply.

It was past midnight and cold when they knew the dragon had left Zandour at last—surely to bring destruction elsewhere. Winged horses lay dead in a heart-rending loss that made men mourn them sick with agony. The disheartened troops huddled, tending wounds, burying their dead. In far-flung towns, RilkenDal's officers tethered their winged mounts and bound their wings so they could not fly away, then forced the townsfolk to build up fires and bring drink and food and pleasures, and soon they were laughing and drunk and sacking what little was left of farms and homes.

Five of Zandour's seven Seers lay dead.

THE DRAGON MOVED through watery moonlight licking blood from his lips. Kish, astride him, was silent, heavy with the satisfaction of killing. He swept soundlessly above Aybil, then down over Farr toward where Kish's cults were camped. "Go to the dark tower," Kish said. "My leaders will come to me there." Both, replete with battle, wanted little more now than a light sleep, perhaps a few moments of mutual pleasure. But suddenly Kish stiffened. Her excitement surged, she could feel Dracvadrig's senses come alert as he reached out to increase control of the girl. For the girl had gone alone—of her own volition—into the citadel and was very close now to taking the stone. They could see her figure, thin and wispy in the moonlight where she stood beside the granite table, staring at the runestone.

Dracvadrig shook off the last vestiges of the drug with effort and brought his power around the girl, enticing her, cajoling her until at last, at last they watched her lift the stone and begin to strip away the gold thread from which it hung. But then almost at once she faltered, hesitated, nearly dropped the stone. Kish sighed impatiently. Dracvadrig strained, pouring his will into her, forcing her until all reluctance was swept away at last, until aggression replaced that reluctance.

She jerked the gold cord away, and clutching the stone, she ran the length of the citadel to the portal and to the balcony there. The mare who waited ducked her head as Meatha leaped astride digging in her heels, then the winged creature swept out into the wind, lifting, banking across the heavy wind to turn westward, coming back over the land; but coming too slowly, hesitating now, reluctant. And Meatha in turn, at the mare's reluctance, began again to grow hesitant.

Dracvadrig eased the girl's mind, soothed her, brought her on toward Pelli artfully until at last she crouched between the mare's wings complacent in her righteousness, lulled by the knowledge that she alone would save Ere. She urged the mare on with authority, pressed her on in spite of the mare's stubbornness. And as Dracvadrig lured the girl, he began at the same time to circle Aybil's dark tower. The stone was theirs now. Soon they would have the second stone. Soon all of Ere would lie at their feet. Already Zandour was done for, and next Pelli would fall, then Farr, Aybil, Sangur. And then —then they would destroy Carriol, with greatest pleasure.

Dracvadrig came down atop the broken tower. His reaching feet knocked away broken stone walls so stone tumbled and clattered onto the old iron bed in the top room of the tower, open now to the sky. More stone fell into the black lake from which the tower rose. Along the shore of the lake, the cults slept peacefully.

ZEPHY AND THORN, restless, shaken by the vision of Zandour, slept at last, but for what seemed only moments before the winged ones near camp spoke to them. Thorn felt Zephy stir. He rose and lit the lamp. She stared up at him vaguely, her brown eyes huge with sleep, then roused herself and sat up. She had been dreaming of Meatha. She shared the disturbing vision with him, but it fled quickly before the urgent voices of the winged ones. *The dragon comes. The warrior queen comes. The dragon sits atop the tower like a buzzard, the dragon that killed our brothers.*

They Saw the dragon hunched atop the tower. *It must wait until dawn,* Thorn said. *I would battle it in daylight, not in darkness. Even with the Seeing, not in darkness.*

Yes, the winged ones said, *it will sleep now. See, it is turning itself back into a man. It will lie with the woman there, and we will keep watch.*

Zephy let the vision of the dragon go. She felt the more urgent vision was with Meatha. She let it flood her mind once more. Thorn felt her distress, took her hand, and sat calmly and silently sorting until at last he had joined her in the vision, knew her alarm as she watched the mare Michennann wing through the night sky, heading straight for Pelli, Meatha sitting straight and tense between her beating wings. "What is she . . ." Zephy began. "What does she carry? What . . . ?"

"The stone!" Thorn said with sudden conviction, gripping her hand so tightly she winced. "Zephy, she has the stone, she has taken it from the citadel."

"The runestone? But she can't, she—"

He stood up and hung the lamp from the tentpole. Light

caught across his red hair, across his bare chest. He looked down at her, still scowling with disbelief and anger.

"The master Seer would never let her," she said stupidly. "Never send one alone. . . ." She did not want to believe what he was telling her. She looked up at him until at last she had to believe. She tried to touch Meatha's mind and to know Meatha's intent.

She could sense great calmness from Meatha, a sense of rightness, a sure purposeful feeling that what she was doing was necessary and right, was essential to the salvation of Ere. She Saw truth in Meatha's purpose: she knew well enough that the master Seers would never let the stone leave Carriol —knew in this moment so close with Meatha, that to carry the stone into battle, to wield it in battle, as Ramad of the wolves had once done, and with it vanquish the Kubalese troops and their dark companions, might be the only sure way to stop the slaughter and to destroy Kubal. She felt uneasy at the theft of the stone, but she felt with Meatha the urgency and rightness, too. She looked up at Thorn. He was watching her intently. They must trust Meatha for a little while, bear with her for a little while. Give her fair chance, not withhold their trust from her. Not yet.

Thorn gave her a questioning look, nodded at last, then blew out the lamp and lay down beside her. Almost at once he was snoring. Zephy scowled at the ease with which he slept, and she lay worrying for a long time. *Should* she alert the council? Thorn had withheld his judgment in this in deference to her. She felt unease at the strength of Meatha's power. And yet if Meatha were right, if the fate of Ere could lie in that one stone carried into battle—Zephy sighed and tossed and could not sleep. And knew, beneath all her arguments, that she must be silent at least for a while. She could not do otherwise. She could not betray Meatha so easily.

She slept at last, restlessly, tossing, then woke again before dawn to find Thorn wakeful beside her, both of them gripped as one in a vision that lifted and excited them, and brought hope. They Saw sleek, fast-running shapes slipping into Zandour and felt the sense of them lusting to destroy the dark warriors: wolves, flowing into the ravaged villages, seeking out the drunken, sated Kubalese troops and killing them. Dozens of wolves killing silently then moving on to kill again.

DRACVADRIG THE MAN sat atop the broken tower seething at the vision of wolves. Wolves! Great Urdd how he hated wolves. Fury overwhelmed him at their slaughter of RilkenDal's troops. They could not waste troops on wolves. Writhing with fury, he grew nearly without volition into the dragon form, forgot the girl who slept among boulders there on the sea cliff, forgot Kish sleeping in the iron bed near him, thought only of the destruction of wolves. Hunched atop the tower, he spread his wings onto the night sky and leaped into darkness to circle once then head for Zandour; left Kish sleeping.

He came down on Zandour screeching with such fury that the very dawn seemed made of dragon screams, swept low back and forth above the hills. But below him lay only emptiness. No wolves to be sensed or seen. Nothing. He dove and raked to death a dozen surviving Zandourian troops and their mounts and tore apart their camp, but his heart wasn't in it. He could think only of wolves and of his own thwarted fury. He snatched one of the horses aloft and carried it back toward Pelli sucking its blood as he flew, crushing it in his terrible anger.

He returned to the tower to consume the rest of it, spitting the heavier bones into the lake below. The sound of his eating soon woke Kish. She stared at him, half with repugnance, half with fascination, as the horse's head disappeared. "So you save the head for last."

He smiled a bloody smile and sat digesting horse in silence, hating the wolves in secret. Where had they come from, those cursed wolves?

Kish said nothing, but as she watched him eating, she

felt his thwarted fury growing around her. She slipped inside the armor of his blocking as cleverly as the serpent slips between stones. She sat quiet, soon Seeing his thoughts clearly. "Wolves!" she hissed. "How did they come without your knowing! How did you let them! Why didn't you . . . ?"

He was sated with horse, his belly distended, in no mood for a tirade. He hunched up across the top of the tower in his haste to be away from her, snarled at her once, then launched himself heavy as lead. He would find somewhere else to digest his breakfast, where he could have peace and silence.

WHEN DRACVADRIG did not return, Kish went down through the dark tower, treading ancient stone stairs around and around past tiers of battered cells where bones lay rotting inside. The drawbridge was down, lying broken and crooked across the black water.

Soon she had passed through the ancient wood and stood at the far edge, surveying her encampments beneath a muddy sky. She saw the four hide tents that housed Carriol's Seers, but she went not to those tents, but to the tall elaborate bower that her people had raised for her.

There she dressed herself in the finery kept ready for her, then called the cultists out of sleep to gather before her. The queen was come, the warrior queen. After ordering the Carriolinian Seers bound and brought to her, she stood scowling impatiently, waiting for her orders to be carried out, for the cultists hardly stirred. They seemed as confused and mindless as a batch of chidrack. What was the matter with them! Only a handful moved toward the Carriolinian tents, then even they were held back forcibly by their neighbors. Kish stared at them unbelieving, then brought powers down on them that sent them to their knees. But still they would not move to fetch the Seers. Their eyes blazed with the old reverence when they looked on Kish, but they would not do her bidding.

And in their tents, knowing what she intended, Zephy and Thorn and the twelve strong young Seers brought their powers, in turn, against Kish. They had been building for this: nursing the sick, conjuring magical ceremonies, doing everything they could to win the awe and love of the cultists. Now they joined together in all their power, in an effort so strong it might not be long expended, but that *must* wed the cults to the light while it held.

Again Kish made her subjects kneel, flashing pain through them. But some rose in spite of the pain and moved toward her. Alarmed, she spoke out in silence to Dracvadrig: she would bring the dragon here and see them all dead before they defied her!

But Dracvadrig did not answer her. He had gone on to the north, beyond Zandour, where now he glided above the high desert, immersed in the hunt like a harrying kestrel, searching over the hot sands and into shadows for wolves, and he had no time for Kish and her toys.

The cultists watched Kish coldly. Her power locked and held against the power of Carriol's Seers. Neither gave. She strained harder until at last, two dozen men broke from the ranks and joined her, taking up weapons to face the rest. But the Carriolinians' power in those brief moments was strong indeed. Who would have thought a handful of Seers . . . ? She needed the power of a runestone. Then she would make the cultists crawl. Blast Dracvadrig for not coming to help her. He could have fetched his stone here, could . . . . Well she would have a runestone all right, a runestone much nearer than the one Dracvadrig carried. Maybe even two stones. And with that power she could destroy the puerile Seers. Yes, perhaps she could retrieve the second stone too, she thought smiling, for already the girl Meatha crouched among boulders watching the divers prepare to bring it up out of the sea.

In a hastily conjured ceremony, Kish appointed new leaders from the few faithful, then she had a horse brought.

Dressed in her finery, mounted, she made the beast rear and roll its eyes, spun it, bid the cultists kneel again before her, then with effort she laid a fog upon their minds like glittering mist so only her face was clear amidst shifting images. She held the vision strong. When at last it faded and the cultists looked up, she was gone.

Chapter
Seven

THE BOULDERS HID MEATHA where she crouched, blocking, staring down the steep drop of sea cliff to where Alardded's camp lay huddled on a narrow shelf just above the sea: two tents, a campfire. The sea was so clear she could see the submerged cliff wall sheering away deep into the water. The diving suit lay like a bloated body next to Alardded's tent, lines coiled beside it. She could sense Michennann grazing inland, but the mare did not speak to her. The whole journey had been conducted in silence, Michennann barely cooperating, reluctant and unpleasant, as Meatha had never known her.

She watched young Roth help Nicoli into the diving suit. Already the divers sensed the stone down there somewhere deep beneath the sea, and so did she. She blocked cautiously to protect the stone she carried, tied in a cloth bag beneath her tunic; waited patiently while Nicoli was dressed like a great doll in the diving suit, and the lines were checked. If she felt the touch of another mind, she turned away and blocked from it. Zephy must bear with her now and trust her if ever their friendship meant anything. Who had more right to the stone than she who had found it? Who had more right than she to carry it in a final battle of powers against the slave-making Kubalese! She held her breath as Nicoli moved slowly to the edge of the cliff then jumped suddenly far out away from the lip. The lines coiled out smoothly after her as Alard-ded tended them, and Roth pumped on the bellows. Meatha grew so interested she soon forgot to block. Alarmed, she touched the stone, brought power around it quickly, chided herself for not paying attention. She watched the circle of bubbles where Nicoli had vanished and thought of the story of Ramad falling into the sea from the back of the monster Hape, of the stone falling away from him there, to be lost— to lie for six generations. How could Nicoli find the stone there, even with Seer's senses to guide her, so small a stone in that immense surging body of water? It seemed to Meatha an impossible task.

Already she could feel that the sea floor was a tumble of boulders. Already she was beginning to know the constriction, the first touch of panic, that the weight and confinement of the sea could bestow. The water rolled around the lines in gentle green swells. She saw through Nicoli's eyes, at first only green light growing darker, then the dark waving shapes of sea plants, a rising boulder, and the underwater world growing constantly darker and closer until Meatha's pulse was pounding with the sense of confinement, the constriction of the heavy suit. The sea was a tomb closing over her. She began to tremble. She blocked frantically, incredulous that Nicoli felt no fear.

She tried to remind herself that it was the lasting curse of the MadogWerg making her feel like this. Don't let it! Don't let it do this to you! But she couldn't seem to help herself. She thought fleetingly that perhaps the MadogWerg had left other weaknesses. Did something dark touch her mind through that weakness, that emptiness she sometimes knew? But no! Nothing touched her but her own resolve, her own commitment to the salvation of Ere. Any other thought was madness. She put all else away from her.

It seemed a long time but was perhaps only minutes before Nicoli drew close among the tumbled, drowned boulders to where the stone lay, its power on her rocking her senses. Meatha felt Nicoli move quickly in the almost total darkness to a narrow cleft between stones, pulling her air line to keep it free; felt her kneel in the cumbersome suit and reach into the cleft. Meatha fought the fear of being trapped. Her hands were sweating. Frantically she blocked to keep from being discovered, tried to calm herself, felt a deeper power give her strength and knew it must be her own power before untapped. She sensed Nicoli reaching, touching. . . . Then she felt the sudden shock in Nicoli's fingers as she touched the stone.

Nicoli grasped it in a handful of sand and pebbles and brought it close to her face. She could see it only as a vague shape through the small, thick glass, but its presence in her hand was like a pulsing heartbeat of power. Meatha felt as if the stone held within itself the thunder of the sea. She felt as if her own hands were on the ropes as Nicoli began to ascend, the runestone tucked safely into her diving suit.

DRACVADRIG SMILED with fine satisfaction. They had the stone. His frustration at searching uselessly across the cursed desert for vanished wolves was as nothing now. The stone was at this moment being carried to the surface of the sea. It was safe, ready to be plucked, ready to be given. He had only to guide and protect Meatha, reassure her, help her to slip the stone away from the divers at the right moment and bring it to him. Then she and the wretched young Seer would begin the final act. Oh yes, soon, soon—as a dragon measures time —the runestone would be whole again, be his, all power would be his.

Meanwhile he must settle Kish. He could not have *her* taking the stone, tampering with his plans. He swept fast along the coast out of Karra and across the Bay of Pelli above the sunken islands and came at Pelli from the sea, but low and on the west coast, so he would remain unseen by the divers around on the southern cliffs. He sensed Kish, then soon saw her riding hard. She had crossed the inlet by barge and was already on the high meadows. He dove on her and saw her horse rear and twist in terror, too frightened even to run. *Turn back, Kish. Leave the horse, my dear, and come onto my back as you were meant to travel.*

"Why should I! You would not help me when I wanted you, why should I heed you now! Go on about *your* warring, worm, and leave me to mine!"

His smile was a hideous sight in that evil dragon face with the ruined eye. *Do not resist me, Kish. You know you do not want to lose me, I am too fine a lover. Surely you would not want me as your enemy. Come, Kish, come—I will destroy the cults for you if that is what you wish, you do not need the stones for that.* He undulated close around her, so the poor horse nearly fell dead from fright. *Come my love, come Kish.* He caressed her with a scaly coil. *Come my love, we are one in this.* He drew his rough dragon tongue across her neck.

She jerked the horse until its mouth bled and stared up at Dracvadrig in fury. "If we are one in this, why shouldn't I use the stones! I won't have my cults—"

There is no time! The young Seer Lobon has reached the gates and will be captive in moments. I need the stones now, I need to bring the girl there to the cells to him, draw her and the stones there to him. . . .

"You move them like sticks and brittles! It's only a game to you!"

More than a game, Kish. This must be done my way. No one must go near or turn the direction of what has begun until she has the stone—the most delicate part, the theft of the stone from the master Seer, is yet to be consummated. Let the girl be, Kish. Come with me. Watch me lead the girl to the abyss. His voice was low and gentle. *Come with me.* But his claw on her arm was like iron, his coils pressing around her strong enough to break bones. Both knew he could kill her if she did not obey. She shivered. Why couldn't she amass the power to drive Dracvadrig away? Even that artless young Seer had—what powers had he touched in that moment when he leaped at Drac and plunged his sword into the dragon's eye? What powers. . . . ? She shivered again, thrust the thought from her and swung her terrified horse away from the dragon with a brutal jerk; she was afraid of Dracvadrig suddenly, she who was afraid of nothing.

Come, Kish. . . .

"Curse your plan!" she hissed. "Curse the wretched girl, curse your precious stones! If you can't use them for me, then stuff them in your gullet!" She kicked the horse hard; the animal leaped away in panic into a dead run, freed at last from the monster, frothing and half-blind with its fear. But she kicked and reined it back toward the dark tower, not toward the direction of the divers, knowing full well that Dracvadrig would kill her, if only to save face, if she pursued the stones. Curse Drac! She did not like having him against her. She needed . . . yes. RilkenDal. RilkenDal would do her bidding. The dark Seer could be more than useful now. Defeated in Zandour by wolves, sore at such defeat, RilkenDal would welcome a woman's sympathy. Later she could consider how to get the stones and deal with the cults, once she had RilkenDal's forces behind her. And then she would take care of Dracvadrig.

LOBON SENSED the fire ogres massed beyond the cliff. Cold fear touched him. Flame edged the cliff, then the first ogre hulked against the sky. The wolves crouched to leap; he raised his bow and shot; a good shot in the neck, the creature fell and rolled down the cliff dislodging stones as it flailed. Two more ogres appeared above, then half a dozen rounded the bend of the narrow trail ahead. He shot again, the wolves leaped, a wolf cried out with pain from the flaming hide. He faced the fire ogres with sword drawn. They advanced until their heat seared him, flame leaping over their warty hides and froglike faces, their small red eyes flame-veiled like evil coals as they forced in around him. One fell from his sword, another pushed in. He slashed and parried, and they were so thick now they were as impregnable as a wall, closing in, stepping across their dead brothers, reaching with flaming hands. He was grappled from behind with burning hands, felt the desperate battling of the wolves with more pain than his own, for they could not attack without being burned; felt chains hot as fire forced around him. He fought the chains until an ogre struck him, and he knew no more.

He woke staring at cell bars. His weapons were gone. The wolves were chained to the wall. On the ground beside him lay the deerskin pouch, charred and torn open. He reached for it, searching uselessly for the runestones, knowing what he would find. He shook it, then lay cursing silently.

But when he felt in his tunic for the wolf bell, its familiar shape cleaved to his hand. He drew it out and stared at it. How had they missed the wolf bell?

They did not miss it, Lobon. Feldyn told him. *They touched it, and it sent pain through them. We have powers in the bell, too, son of Ramad. And we know a hate for the fire ogres perhaps surpassing your own. Though we had not enough power to keep them from chaining us.* The black wolf lay looking across at Lobon, fettered by chains, bleeding and weak with pain. Lobon pulled himself up and went to examine Feldyn's wounds.

The chains binding the wolves had been locked to bolts in the wall. The smell of singed hair was strong. All three wolves were burned, but much of the burn was hair, not deep into the skin. He looked for his waterskin and saw it at last lying some distance outside the cell bars, charred black. The ground was wet where it had been dumped.

MEATHA CURLED DOWN in her shelter of boulders to wait for deeper night. She was glad the sky was cloudy, for dusk had come more swiftly. Alardded's campfire smelled so good, and supper smelled even better. She munched on cold mountain meat and waited. The drowned stone lay so close, just there in Alardded's pack.

It had been nearly a day since she left Carriol. Was the illusion she had created in the citadel, of a runestone hanging there, working so well that still no one suspected? When she thought of the powers she had been capable of these last days, she could hardly believe it was all her own doing. Yet what else could it be? She *felt* the power in herself. If her illusion held, if they thought the stone was still in the citadel—just until she could slip into Alardded's camp, retrieve that second stone, slip away to join the battles in Farr and Aybil, banish the darkness there—if only her image of the false stone would hold so she would not be followed. She put her head on her knees and dozed, waiting for those below to sleep, holding her blocking tight around her, secure in the goal she pursued, secure in her love for Carriol.

LOBON'S HANDS were bloody from scraping against stone where he had been digging at Shorren's chain. He had dug late into the night, and when at last Shorren pulled herself free with a final lunge, the twin moons were low, casting shadows through the cell bars. The white wolf had slunk away deep into the cave to the trickle of water Lobon had found, dragging her chain behind her. Lobon stared down at the rock in his hands, then he began to dig anew, at Feldyn's chain. Crieba lay patiently waiting his turn. Lobon tried not to think that they could die here, with two wolves still chained to the wall. He tried not to remember that the sense of Drac-vadrig he had followed to the cell had been a trap, just as the wolves had said. That if he had listened to them, none of them would be captive now behind a barred, locked gate.

He continued to dig. The digging stones kept breaking, and his fingers were raw. When the wolves' thirst grew too great, he went into the inner caves and let his cupped hands slowly fill with water from the small warm trickle there and brought it out to them, making the trip over and over. Shorren brought water in her mouth and let them suck it up.

Once as he dug at the stone he Saw an image of the girl, her beautiful face rapt in some vision he was unable to share, her lavender eyes deep and intent, very determined as if she contemplated something demanding, though he could not make out what. He felt clearly her rising excitement.

Why did such visions touch him? Whatever she was about, whatever vision she cleaved to, had nothing to do with him. Her dark lashes were soft on her cheeks, her dark hair tumbled about her shoulders. Her eyes held him so strongly that he thought she Saw him; but then she rose preoccupied, unaware of anything but the turmoil within herself. She pulled off her boots and slipped barefoot out of the rock shelter where she had been sitting, into the moonlight, and began to move carefully down a steep cliff. He could hear the sea crashing. He saw her destination: a camp below on a rocky ledge. When she reached it at last, she stood watching the two tents, sensing out. Finally she approached the larger one, still in silence, and he could feel her blocking.

How could he See her when she blocked so strongly? He frowned, puzzling. Did he have some special affinity for this girl, to so breach her blocking? Some tie with her that he did not understand? She approached the tent and entered in silence. He sensed rather than saw the two sleeping figures, and startled, for a master Seer slept there. And a boy, also with Seer's skills. The girl knelt beside the master Seer and began to feel with light, quick fingers among his belongings, quickly touched something of power that made him start and catch his breath.

She pulled the runestone out of the pack, he felt the weight and power of it as if he held it himself. A shard of the runestone of Eresu.

Now she had two shards, he thought, puzzling. What

was so urgent to this girl? What exactly did she plan? He watched her retreat softly and climb the cliff. He felt her silent call, then felt the answering call and saw a winged mare bank between clouds and plummet down beside her out of the moonwashed sky; and he felt the strange reluctance of the mare. The girl swung onto her back and nearly at once they were windborne, the girl prodding, forcing the mare. He wanted to move with them, to follow. What was the girl's destination, carrying the runestones? She seemed to imagine something urgent, but her intention was muddled and confused in his mind. He tried to follow her in vision, but his thoughts remained fixed above the cliff as mare and rider disappeared into moon-touched cloud.

He had started to turn from the vision of the empty cliff when he Saw the other rider standing motionless beside a winged stallion. How could he have missed them, missed sensing them? Had they come out of the sky unseen only a moment before? Or had they been standing hidden by boulders watching the girl just as he himself had watched her? A tall, thin man with short white hair. The sight of him struck a cord of recognition in Lobon, though he could not think why. He didn't know him. There was a power about him, a mystery about him that drew Lobon. The stranger stood looking into the sky where girl and mare had disappeared with a cold, impersonal censure. Then in one leap he was mounted and following.

DRACVADRIG CLUNG in resting coils around the peak of Scar Mountain, drawing the girl to him, watching the mare wing through the night sky, pulled inexorably by his power and by the power RilkenDal had laid so beautifully upon her. Even should the girl turn reluctant, the mare would not waver from the hold they now had on her. And where better to receive the stones than here atop Scar Mountain, where Ramad had been bred and born, then snatched away from his rightful destiny as a child of the dark masters? Now the stone would return to dark. Here, where it had first been betrayed.

Never mind how the warring fared across the coastal countries, it didn't matter now, with this tender Seer girl to seal the fate of Ere. He smiled a toothy smile against the dark sky. Oh yes, the girl would seal Ere's fate—but not in the way she dreamed. To drive back the dark? Oh no, young woman! Dracvadrig chuckled, a sound like grinding bones. Not to drive back the dark, but to breed an heir to the dark. An heir to the joining of the runestone.

His eye began to pain him. He pawed at it absently, never taking his mind from his prey. Here on Scar Mountain had Ramad been bred out of cold revenge. Here this night the girl would come, she in turn to be bred—to begin a new line of Seers that would be heir to Ramad. Heir to the joining of the stones.

Seers subservient to him alone, and to the dark powers.

For something had been building for generations and it was culminating now. His own quickening to life there in the abyss was witness to that building of powers. Powers growing in force, powers of the earth itself as natural as the volcanoes that belonged to them, or the sly movement of the moons; and other powers wrought of the minds of living creatures—forces *men* called good and evil. Forces that moved like winds, shifting, violent, that even he, Dracvadrig, did not always anticipate.

Forces that could split Ere's plane of life apart, could open it to other planes. Already there was a wound in the fabric of this plane: there the Luff'Eresi dwelt. If Ere's plane should so shatter, as the stone had once shattered, then when it opened to new planes, those *must* be the planes of the dark. And if such violence should not occur? Oh but the dark could force such holocaust, if it had the stone, joined in darkness. And the dark powers would then own Ere.

No matter his scoffing at the joining when he faced young Lobon, that joining was now too opportune to ignore.

And it must be for the dark. And only an heir to Ramad could so join it.

This girl, coming to him now as docile as a ewe, would make that heir for him. An heir far more tractable, more obedient, than ever the difficult young Lobon could be. He soothed the girl and beckoned her on, and she drew ever closer. Then suddenly his senses stirred uncomfortably. Scowling, he felt out across the night sky, parting winds, reaching—and he Saw suddenly the white-haired Seer following close behind the girl, riding tall between a dark stallion's wings. *A white-haired Seer!* Dracvadrig spat fire, pawed the stony peak with fury. Where had this man come from! Why were the white-hairs not gone from Ere! Surely he and Kish had destroyed them. His snarl of rage rose to a scream against the lonely night. It was the white-haired one called Anchorstar, the same who had led the Children of Ynell from Burgdeeth, who had led Ramad outside of Time—that one would die this time. He wanted to spring into the sky; but he remained steady, drawing the girl, and with her the white-haired one, closer.

THE MARE FLEW strongly toward the northwest. Meatha did not wonder when Michennann ceased to resist her, when the mare began to beat steadily across the night wind. She thought only that she had bested Michennann at last.

She could sense new movements of Kubalese troops, knew she must come down on them there in the north, drive them back with the power of the stones. She must circle the coastal countries, destroy every Kubalese soldier as only the power of the stones could destroy them. She was the stones' willing servant now in this last, this all-decisive attack. She was very sure, very aware of her power; so engulfed in the aura of that power that she did not sense the presence following her. She turned to look back only when Michennann faltered, touched with sudden fear.

She looked back beneath Michennann's wings, sensed

the man suddenly and sharply, then saw him: tall and slim he sat the dark, winging mount, white hair gleaming, and her first response was sudden wild joy at knowing he was alive, he whom she had mourned.

Then fear swept her as it had swept Michennann. And then shame. His censure was sharp as a sword.

But why was she ashamed? He had no right to make her feel ashamed. He should be pleased, should be helping her. She felt amazed and hurt. Why didn't he understand? She tried to touch his thoughts and met only coldness and disdain. She urged the mare faster, appalled at his insensitiveness, he who had always understood. Dracvadrig's power pulled at her, and she followed blindly, needing that power now in her loneliness, pushing back wildly the suspicion that was beginning to awaken within her deepest thoughts.

She was over the north of Zandour. She would turn now and come low onto the Kubalese troops, bring the power of the stones down on them. She spoke to the mare in silence, laid a hand on her neck, urging her into a low sweep over Zandour.

But the mare would not turn or lower her wings to sweep down, would not speak or acknowledge her command. She simply continued north, ignoring Meatha's bidding. Meatha glanced back at Anchorstar. This was his doing! How could he! She brought her power strong against Michennann, against Anchorstar, and was ignored by both. Michennann would not turn aside, would not speak to her, the mare was caught in a mindless pull northward. How could Anchorstar not understand? She wanted to scream at him and make him draw away.

She tried again to make Michennann turn, but felt only a dull blank fixedness of mind quite unlike the mare, unlike any winged one. She slapped Michennann's neck, jerked her mane; all uselessly. Michennann kept on, caught in a web, now, beyond her will, beyond her ability to destroy.

It was then Anchorstar gave her the vision. It seemed to have nothing to do with her plight, with the dilemma engulfing her. She saw five people, all white-haired, one of them a child. One was Anchorstar. One was Tra. Hoppa. Another woman. A young man. They stood in a meadow greener than the jade itself. Behind them rose a strange, clear dome. It looked as if it were made of glass, though that would be impossible; glass was made only in very small pieces. It might have been formed of crystal out of the mountains, so strange it was. There was a sense of power and warmth, of rightness; a sense of other things gone too quickly to grasp.

When the vision left her, her mind seemed to clear from a confusion she had hardly been aware of. The warmth and rightness of that place, the sense of power, remained with her; but part of the vision escaped too quickly, was gone. Now she felt clear-headed, as if she had awakened from a nightmare where all her senses had been awry. She knew suddenly and completely, with a shock that chilled her, that she had never been meant to reach the Kubalese troops. That she had never been meant to destroy those troops. She knew, as sharply as if her face had been slapped, that she and Michennann were being led toward a different destination. Toward a destination filled with terror. She turned to stare back at Anchorstar, crying out to him now for help, knowing he meant only to show her the truth. . . .

And he was gone from the sky. Gone as if he had never been there.

She was alone with a truth she did not want, fighting Michennann to turn aside—fighting too late to alter her own dark course; and Michennann caught and held utterly now, to some stronger will. Michennann, left too long to battle alone, had lost that battle. Meatha's fear turned to terror. She clung, stricken, to the silent, fast-flying mare. She saw now that the very stealing of the runestones had been willed by the dark she had meant to defeat. Now she saw, and now it was too late. Now she battled a mare caught herself in forces beyond her will. Meatha tried, but could not reach the mare's spirit. She strained to bring power through the stones and seemed weak and inept. She tried to make the mare end their flight in a fast spiraling downward, but Michennann did not heed her, was led on like a bird snared in flight. Why had Anchorstar turned away? Why hadn't he helped her? She was sick and trembling. She could smell the mare's nervous sweat. Something urged them to greater speed still, and neither she nor Michennann could resist.

And Lobon woke shouting into empty blackness, "Fight him! Fight Dracvadrig! The power of the bell is with you!" He turned and saw the wolves sitting erect in their chains and felt their power steadily rising with his own to strengthen the girl and drive the firemaster back. He tried with all his power to give her the strength she sought. Dracvadrig *must not* have the runestones she carried. He did not think about why he cared, why this was important to him.

And his power was not enough, the mare was buffeted until she faltered in the sky; and then suddenly the dragon launched himself from the peak of Scar Mountain and swept toward them, black against the stars, driving winds aside. He came at them, slashed at the mare and pale rider forcing them on not only with mind-power but with teeth like steel, with claws that were knives, with a frenzy of beating wings. The mare fought to keep airborne. Meatha lashed out with her sword again and again, but the mare was forced down at last toward the abyss by the dragon's leathery wings beating across her wings. Lobon Saw blood smeared across the dragon's face, and he did not know he was shouting again, sending power like a tide from the wolf bell. He tore in rage at the bolt that held Feldyn, and the wolf leaped and leaped in frustration, then suddenly came free, the bolt clanging to the floor as the mare and girl were swept down the side of the abyss. The dragon dove, snatched the girl up in its claws, and beat skyward carrying her like a cloth doll. Lobon felt her quick decision to drop the stones and cried out to her. He made her pause and close her fist over them, perplexed.

Then he saw, not in vision but against the night sky beyond the cell, the dragon's dark shape come out of the wind swooping down past the cell dangling the girl. He saw her face for an instant, pale with fear, her cheek torn and bloody. She lashed out again with the sword, then the dragon was gone with her. Lobon sensed it entering a red-washed cave, Saw fire ogres moving inside. One snatched a cloth bag from the girl and pushed her against the wall; she screamed with the pain of the burns it left on her wrist and shoulder; Lobon could feel that pain. The cloth sack where she had carried the two runestones was aflame. The fire ogre picked the two stones out and laid them on top a flat boulder. Lobon saw then that his own two shards, and the starfires, lay there gleaming red with reflected fire. He watched the dragon inspect the stones, then watched as a fire ogre swept them up in its thick flaming hand and tumbled them into the golden casket that dangled at the dragon's throat.

The dragon left the cave carrying six shards of the runestone of Eresu. Lobon could hear it scraping across loose stone, then heard boulders dislodged, and was engulfed in the sense of it close by. The night turned red as ogres approached. They fumbled with the lock, and the dragon's heavy blackness covered the stars beyond the cell. The gate was pulled open.

The dragon pushed through the cell door. Its claws reached for him. He lashed out with the bell down the side of its head, and it hissed and pulled back, coughing flame at him.

Again it reached. Again. As it turned, he saw the left eye swollen closed and covered with dried blood. Each time he struck with Seer's powers and the bell, it retreated, then attacked anew. He could feel the wolves' powers with him, strong. Its jaws opened above him, flame belching to burn him. Its teeth grazed his shoulder. He pressed deeper into the cave; it pushed in after him, pressed so close—but then it drew back. He tried to find a way clear of its coils and was trapped by it.

But it did not attack. It was only toying with him.

Why? Surely it wanted the wolf bell. He stood facing it. It was utterly still, watching him, and the sense of the man Dracvadrig was there, alert and evil. It did not move. It had only to kill him and take the wolf bell, but it did not move. Did it want him alive? But why would it? It seemed to draw back to keep from killing him. Why? It wanted the wolf bell, though. It stared at it greedily. He reached out desperately to any power that could help him. The creature remained utterly still. He felt the wolves with him, felt more than these three wolves; knew suddenly that wolves in a great band pushed their power like a heavy tide to buoy him; and he felt the girl where she stood captive, fighting beside him. Then suddenly Feldyn and Shorren leaped and slashed at it, their chains dragging, Shorren on one side, Feldyn on the other, ducking flame; the dragon moved now, swept this way and that trying to see them, to get at them. Its eye seemed to pain it. Its coils lashed the walls, the golden pouch at its throat swung and gleamed. Lobon tried to turn the power of the stones it carried against it. Could such a thing be done? Did the dark hold that power utterly? He felt the wolves' power strong, so strong. He brought his skills, his knowledge to bear as perhaps he never had before; the sense of those other wolves somewhere, somewhere, reaching out to give him power twisted something in Lobon, brought the sense of Ramad around him sharply. He forced and drove down on the dragon with the power that rose in him married to those other powers. The dragon took a step back, slowed in its battling and swung its head. Lobon exalted in his power and in the fellowship of wolves. He leaped suddenly with the wolf bell at the dragon's head, slashed the bell across its cheek, then leaped and struck the damaged eye; the dragon bellowed out with pain, with fury. It writhed, blood gushed from the eye; and then, writhing, its body began to grow unclear.

Twisting and bellowing, it diminished in size as if the pain were too great to let it hold the dragon form. He felt it reaching to strengthen its power in the stones it carried, felt it falter as those powers that buoyed Lobon confused and rattled its mind; Powers stood beside Lobon now—Skeelie's, the wolves—that awed and humbled him. The dragon diminished further. It had begun to change into the form of a man. The two forms overlapped and wavered. The bones seemed to shrink, to draw in.

At last the man Dracvadrig stood before him, tall and bent and sallow, his lined face filled with hate. The gold casket dangled across his waist. One eye gushed blood. The other was a dragon's eye, predatory and cold.

I have not moved out of the realm of Canoldir's house and out of this Timeless place, to help Lobon. I am uncertain what to do. Perhaps Canoldir is right, perhaps I must wait. Must Lobon fight his battles unfettered? Would my interference unbalance the scales of what is, turn away the delicate balance of powers, and perhaps destroy that balance?

What am I to do? Do the Luff'Eresi watch Lobon and the warring upon Ere? Surely they care. From what Ram told me, they care more than we can know. But they put their feelings aside in deference to man's free-choosing.

Must I continue to wait, then? Is this what they, all wise, would tell me? Yet I suffer for Lobon. And I fear for Ere. .

In my fearing, should I not move to help? Must I not tip the balance? Am I not a part of that balance any more, since I move outside of Time? Yet if I do not go to him, will I shatter all hope?

If I could have a vision of the Luff'Eresi as I had once long ago, if a word from their greater wisdom could guide me. . . .

But they will not tamper with the affairs of men. It is up to me to decide.

And I do not know what to do.

From the Journal of Skeelie of Carriol
Undated. Marked only, *The Villa of Canoldir.*

Part Three

The Joining

Chapter Eight

BEYOND ESH-NEN, beyond Time, in the villa of Canoldir, Skeelie stood staring into the dying fire, but Seeing only Lobon facing the firemaster. The dragon had changed to the form of a man. The wolf bell was bloodied, and Lobon's dark eyes were blazing with hatred. She remembered sharply how Ramad had faced the master of Urdd, twelve years gone, felt again Ram's anger. Her hand clutched convulsively at her sword as she felt again the pain of Ram's death. "I must go to Lobon now. I must."

"You cannot help him, Skeelie. Not any more than he can help himself." Canoldir stood tall in darkened leathers before the stone mantel, taut with the visions and with her fierce need. His dark eyes caressed her, were filled with forces and wonders no woman could turn away from.

She drew a breath, watching him. "I must go to him. I *can* help him. I must be beside him to try."

"Part of the force that drives you, Skeelie, is guilt. Because you were not beside Ramad to help him."

She stared at him defiantly, knowing he was right.

"You think your Seer's powers were not enough alone to save Ram, and now too late you would battle with your sword." His look was uncompromising. "The sword alone will never be sufficient to destroy such as Dracvadrig. Try your Seer's powers now, Skeelie. You have more than you know."

"My power is not enough without the sword. You must let me go to him."

"Perhaps I will not be able to bring you back. My own powers. . . ." Their shared look was long and expressed their shared needs. *I cannot let you go without tearing my soul from me.*

"You must let me go. I cannot see him die as Ram died. Nor can I see the stones remain with the dark Seers. Nor—nor can *you.*"

"The fates will have their way regardless of what we do."

"You do not believe that. You know you do not. Let me go. I will come back to you. I must come back to you. The Luff'Eresi—"

"The Luff'Eresi care nothing for this. They would not lift a finger to help."

"They helped Ram once. To save the Children of Ynell. You do not believe what you say! You can't turn away from the stones—from Ere—uncaring."

I care only for you. He took her by the shoulders, pulled her to him. But she held the vision of Lobon facing the master of Urdd and would not yield to the gentleness of his touch or to his lonely need.

DRACVADRIG'S VOICE was dry as wind. His form, diminished from dragon to man, seemed only the more horrifying in its sparsity and sepulchral stance. He took a sword from a fire ogre's hand, and it reflected the flame of the ogre's face red as blood. "Now I will have the bell, son of a bastard!" The firemaster's power was the power of all darkness. Crieba leaped at his chain. Feldyn and Shorren crouched snarling, then lurched forward dragging their chains to stand beside Lobon, tensed to spring. Dracvadrig stood hunched as a bird of prey, sword poised, then moved forward. Lobon did not step back, was wild with the power in him, the power of that great pack of wolves, the power of the girl in a strange warm closeness; he raised the wolf bell and felt another power and exalted, felt Skeelie there with him; he knew he could kill Dracvadrig now, at this instant. . . .

KISH'S SWORD was poised against the throat of a peasant, crouching among his dead companions, when the vision of Dracvadrig and Lobon struck her. Somehow, Dracvadrig seemed so small there in the form of a man, dwarfed by the abyss out behind him as if somehow his human form had shrunk. She watched his expression coldly, watched the young Seer; and she knew suddenly and surely that Dracvadrig could die there in the next instant, die in the rising power the young Seer had found. Who was helping him? Curse Carriol and her Seers! She gored the peasant and turned from his fallen body, saw that RilkenDal had already snatched the bridles of two fettered mares of Eresu. She ran, snatched the reins, was mounted. No matter that she hated Dracvadrig, Lobon must not have the stones! They beat and spurred the reluctant animals until the creatures could only leap skyward, were soon pounding the wind in a frenzy of speed under the sharp sting of the whips.

The setting sun sent a streak of crimson along the underside of the clouds, and beneath that bloody sky the dark Seers held steady the vision of Lobon and the firemaster. The young Seer's powers came too strong. They must not allow Dracvadrig's defeat, must not allow the stones to be taken. What powers buoyed the Seer? They sensed a power from the captive girl helping him, other powers; and then Lobon had cornered Dracvadrig.

The bastard's son must not have the stones! RilkenDal pressed his mount until the mare began to slaver, her eyes white with terror. Her wings did not want to hold her, she faltered, seemed ready to fall; he beat her until she strained harder, drove her on toward the abyss.

At last they were over Urdd, the heaving animals stag-

gering against the wind, then dropping from the sky like
stones.

The mares stumbled to the earth and fell on their knees,
their wings splaying along the ground like injured birds. The
riders leaped free and ran. They were too late, they felt Dracvadrig's exhaustion, felt him take a mortal blow and stagger
from the cell, trying in a final bid for power to take the dragon
form, and too weak to muster that power.

"The Seer will have the stones!" Kish hissed, running
hard. She was light on her feet and fast. "Those useless mares
dropped us too far from the cells. Run! For the love of Urdd,
he must not have the stones! Use your power! Help him
change to dragon!"

LOBON FOLLOWED the retreating firemaster into the twilight of
the abyss, Shorren pushing close. Feldyn tried to follow, but
fell, his injured leg and shoulder striking a painful dizziness
to sap his conscious will. Shorren's dragging chain made a
harsh din in the silence; her spirit was predatory, thirsting for
blood.

They found the master of Urdd lying among boulders in
a form half-dragon, half-man, the long tail twisted around
jagged rocks, the human legs half formed. They could feel his
waning powers as he attempted to complete the change. His
breathing was shallow and quick, his face gone in a horrifying
mixture of shapes. The runestones lay scattered beside him,
the broken gold casket smashed beneath the bulk of dragon
shoulder from which protruded a man's puny arm, its claw-
like fingers clutching at his fallen sword.

Lobon jerked the sword from Dracvadrig's hand and
pressed the tip into the firemaster's chest. Then he paused.
He could pierce the firemaster's heart now, he had lived
twelve years for this moment. And suddenly he was numb
with confusion and uncertainty.

Shorren growled; her voice filled his mind. *Kill him! What do you wait for!* She crouched, ready to spring, to tear out Dracvadrig's throat. *Do you lose your nerve, Lobon, after all your bragging talk of how you would destroy the master of Urdd?*

He steadied his hand. Something lost and empty had stirred in him. He fought it back and plunged the sword home deep through dragon's chest and man's. Blood spurted like a river. The bloodied eye stared up at him blindly as the pierced heart ceased to beat.

He knelt beside the creature, half-man half-dragon, mutilated and dead, and picked up a shard of the runestone and wiped the blood from it, retrieved another and another until he held all five and the starfires. Then he turned and stared at Shorren, filled with emotions he dared not examine. She knew. She saw it in him. She looked back at him steadily.

The hatred of a lifetime was satisfied. And the emptiness it left lay a terror on his heart that he did not understand.

Your quest is ended, Lobon. Dracvadrig is dead. Is your reason for being ended too?

He stared at her, puzzled. He did not know how to answer such a question.

Finally he stirred himself, looked again at the tangled body, stiffening now to cleave around boulders in coils and twisted human limbs. Then he began to examine the stones and to read one by one the runes carven into them. But the runes were only scattered words. None, alone, made sense. He started to fit stone to stone, but something made him cease abruptly. He stared down at the stones, puzzling. "What do these words mean, Shorren? What does the whole rune say?"

Shorren did not answer.

He turned and saw her lying sprawled across her chains, her coat wet with seeping blood where a sword protruded from her chest. His shock froze him, he could not speak or cry out. He stared dumbly at the two figures that stood over her, reached out desperately for some contact with Shorren, knowing she was dead. There was no answering touch from her mind, only emptiness; and his mind, his spirit, could not believe that she was dead.

When at last he looked directly at the figures, the sense of them chilled him through. The man was dark-haired and bearded and stood crookedly: a Farrian Seer: this was RilkenDal, surely. The woman was a pale, bloodless creature, watching him as a snake watches its prey. The dark Seers moved suddenly, swords flashed; he parried, fought with terrible fury, wild at the murder of Shorren, wanting to scream out in agony for Shorren. The woman was strong as a man. The two forced him in the direction of the cell; as he struck at the woman, RilkenDal brought a blow across his neck that jarred his vision and flashed hot pain through him.

He knew no more until the woman's cold hands lifted and forced him through the cell door. Half waking, dizzy, he knew she had the stones. He saw Feldyn lying against the cell wall bleeding, saw the woman advance on him then draw back hissing and felt Feldyn's power and Crieba's driving her back. With the last of his strength Lobon forced protection for the wolf bell pressed so painfully against his ribs, and felt the wolves do the same.

She did not come near him again. Her expression alone, he thought, might easily kill. She was white with hatred, her lips pulled back. "We will have the bell soon enough, Ramad's brat!"

She stood beside the dark Seer, just inside the iron gate. In a moment a fire ogre appeared, pushing the girl Meatha ahead of it. She seemed confused, her face flushed from the fire, her arms painfully burned. She glanced at him, pleading, then lowered her gaze. The warrior queen took hold of her arm in a grip that made her wince, and shoved her toward RilkenDal. The Seer steadied his knife against the girl's chest, and the warrior queen lifted her hands and began to draw signs above the girl's head.

"What Dracvadrig began," the warrior queen said, "we

will consummate." Lobon could feel the woman's power, hypnotic and intense. Her incantation was in words foreign to him, in words that soothed him strangely, then made his blood burn hot, brought a wildness leaping in him and a passion that he saw reflected in the girl's face as she turned to look at him. What was this spell? Emotions like flame pummeled him; Meatha's cheeks were flaming; she bent her head as if in shame. A power flowed between them like a river, a yearning between them, the warrior queen's words drowning them in desire; and then they began to understand the words. The woman's voice was low and compelling. "As lovers need, so lovers cleave. And in cleaving bring new life. As Seers need, so Seers cleave. And in cleaving bring more than life: Bring to me blood meant to rule the bell. Bring to me blood meant to join the stone. New blood will join the stone in darkness, join the stone to darkness to hold and to wield beyond challenge."

He was dizzy with desire. Meatha held herself steadier. He watched her, saw her tense suddenly with another emotion sharp and predatory. *Help me, Lobon! Now!* She spun, her silent words shouting in his mind, she struck the warrior queen in the stomach and groin and grabbed her sword, but the woman spun away. Meatha was after her as Lobon snatched up a rock. He closed on RilkenDal as Feldyn passed him, leaping against the man, and together they toppled the dark Seer. Lobon raised the rock to strike, but the man's power stayed him, weakened him; RilkenDal's power closed over his mind so he fought for consciousness and could strike only glancing blows; then he began to drop into blackness, was half conscious of Feldyn tearing at the Seer's throat in a thrashing, bloody combat.

He woke hurting and confused, and looked around him. The cell gates were locked, they were captive. The warrior queen was gone, the sense of her gone. Meatha leaned against the bars, weak with pain. He stared beyond the locked gate into the abyss and saw RilkenDal there lying dead with his throat torn away. He rose and put his arm around Meatha to help her, but the emotion that gripped him made him step back as if he were burned. She looked up at him. "I tried—I tried to get the stones."

He felt against his tunic for the wolf bell and drew it out. "She could not touch the bell," he said quietly, knowing the wolves had protected the bell, feeling their power, the two here in the cave aligned now with the angry power of the great pack that roamed the high desert lands.

But Kish had power, she carried the power of six stones. Still, the fury of the wolves, the passion of the wolves, was greater. He stared at Meatha and knew at last the true importance of the commitment of the stones' bearer. Remorse at the possession of the stones by the dark powers sickened him; he knew now, too painfully, that to avenge Ramad's death was not enough, had never been enough.

"And now it is too late," he said, searching Meatha's face. He turned away from her, torn with self-disgust; but beyond his anguish there was the sense of the warrior queen near to them, he could feel her cruel pleasure in the power she now wielded, felt the strength of the spell she cast and knew he should feel disgust, should know anger, and felt only desire. He needed this girl now, needed her to drive out the storm of self-disgust, didn't care about reason or anger or spells, knew he must hold her, was sick with desire for her. He could see her own desire reflected in her eyes.

"If we are to die at Kish's hand," he whispered, "might we not die together, die close together, as one—

"Stop it, Lobon! Stop it! She doesn't want us to die! Don't you see. She wants. . . ."

"An heir," he said, facing the truth of Kish's plan.

"Yes. An heir. The stone is not yet joined. We must not give her an heir, must not let it be joined as long as it can be held by the dark powers." Her face was flaming, her fear and confusion at the strength of her own desire making her wild with anger. "There must be no heir! There must be no joining of the stone in darkness!"

Still he felt Kish's powers twisting his thoughts.

"Come," she said. "Feldyn needs us." She knelt before the dark wolf, ripped a long hem from her tunic, and began to wipe blood from the wound. "If we had birdmoss, salve. . . ."

He took the bloody rag from her and went deep into the cave, where he rinsed and moistened it. When he returned, she was sitting with Feldyn's head in her lap. He stared down at her, then looked at the locked gate.

He had failed in everything. The stones were gone. Feldyn would die here; all four of them would die. And with the stones gone, Ere was surely defeated. He was dully amazed that he cared—about the stones, about Ere; but he was certain now that Dracvadrig's death was not enough, had never been enough.

Meatha watched him without expression; and when he looked at her, Kish's words rang again between them. *New blood will join the stone in darkness, join the stone to darkness.* Kish was out there somewhere near to them, they could feel her presence couched in the power of the stones.

Meatha sighed and turned back to tending Feldyn. "We must get away from this place."

"And how do you think we can do that? And what good will it do? *She* has the stones. She—"

She gave him a direct, hard look and did not answer. Her eyes were amazing, large and as lavender as the plumage of the mabin bird, her lashes dark and thick. He could not look away again, and now her anger was lost on him. But she kept her distance.

Late in the night as Meatha slept, Lobon rose and stood watching her. He felt the wolves wake, felt their steady gazes, and at last he turned away.

You might be digging, Crieba told him. *I have been patient beyond endurance. I am sick to death of this chain.*

Scowling, Lobon found a stone and began to dig, soon was spending his passion and fury against the rock wall. He dug the rest of night. Sometimes Meatha woke, watched him sleepily, then sighing, slept again. When the abyss beyond the bars began to lighten, he went to press his face against the cold iron to stare upward where, miles above, sun made a gold streak along the rim of the high valley. It was then he saw the charred remains of RilkenDal's body, where the fire ogres had been at it. He heard Crieba leaping against his chain, turned, as with a final lunge the gray wolf pulled the bolt free and slammed shoulder first into Feldyn, who snarled with pain.

The gray wolf went stiffly off to the back of the cave to drink, and to hunt for lizards, just as poor Shorren had done earlier. Not long afterward he returned with three white lizards for Feldyn. As Feldyn ate, Crieba lay licking the dark wolf's wounds. Lobon turned to his stone bed and slept.

He woke with late morning light washing the bars of the cell. Meatha was still sleeping, cradled now against Crieba's shoulder, as if she had been cold. Her dark hair spilled across the wolf's gray coat, her hand lay palm upward across his muzzle. The wolves were wakeful, he could sense their grieving for Shorren, and his own grief rose in a sudden sharp pain. But the wolves grieved differently, for they believed completely that Shorren would live again as her spirit moved in the natural progression of souls. Lobon was not sure. He felt sick at the thought of lovely Shorren lying bloodied and stiff in the abyss.

It was then he felt his mother with him and his emptiness was terrible. He turned his thoughts angrily from her and blocked her out. He did not want to show his emotions to her, show his pain for Shorren or his terrible lusting for Meatha that was no more than the warrior queen's spell.

Show his empty failure, his loss of the stones—the loss of Ere to the dark. *Dracvadrig is dead!* He cried out in spite of himself. *And Ramad is avenged! What more do you want!*

She did not answer him.

Chapter
Nine

KISH TIED THE WINGED MARE near a water lick, though the
stupid animal seemed so sickly she didn't think it would last
long. RilkenDal's mare was already dead. Curse them. Curse
RilkenDal for dying and leaving her here. Curse the bastard
son of Ramad and the wolf bell that clung to him. She would
have that bell and the stone it held! She spilled the shards of
the runestone into her palm, felt their weight, considered
their amassed power, then dropped them back into her tunic.
She must have the other two shards still missing, must find a
way to seek them out. She stared up at the black cliff above
her and at the winged lizards diving mindlessly after birds.
Perhaps, because of the sickly mare, she would have no choice
but to subdue the creatures and somehow bring them down
to her and make them tractable, bad-tempered and stupid as
they were. She had to have some way out of this barren
valley. She wished she had RilkenDal's skill at controlling
stupid beasts. But now, with the power of the stones. . . .

Some distance away on a ridge, the gray mare the girl
had ridden stood watching her. Nasty thing. She tried to lure
it. The power of the stones came strong, exciting her, making
the mare shy and paw and try twice to wheel and fly away,
though caught by the power Kish wielded, its wings were
pinioned as if it were in a snare. But then in one wild surge it
reared and rose, straining in spite of her power, and was gone.

Curse the stupid animal! She stood sulking and furious. Then she pulled the stones from her robe once more and stared down at them.

The power of the stones might not have held the mare, but they wielded a far greater force in battle, for with them she had strengthened the Kubalese warriors until now they drove the Carriolinians back toward Carriol, drove her own ungrateful cults back with them. A handful of cultists remained loyal and fought now beside Kearb-Mattus with a zeal that made her smile with satisfaction.

She shook the stones and watched their green fire flash across her palm. Three more stones to complete the runestone. The wolf bell had been as immovable as if it were fastened to the earth when she tried to lift it from the Seer's tunic. Curse Dracvadrig and RilkenDal both for being dead. She needed their power now. But she *would* have the wolf bell. She must.

She thought with brief speculation of Kearb-Mattus, but he had no Seer's powers to help her, only brute strength. Still he might be a satisfactory lover if nothing more. He was brawny, with a killer's lust she liked. There would be time for play once she had the stones and a human creature bred to the joining. She smiled. Now it would be *her* runestone, whole and powerful. Shared with no one. She would raise the child of Lobon to her ways, and he would do her bidding.

She turned to stare down the long drop of the abyss to where the iron gates held safe her captives. Now there was only to breed them, to get the heir to the stone's final and inevitable joining. She scowled. The girl seemed as without passion as a toad. Blast her. The spell on her had so far only made her avoid the boy like a plague. And that one, Lobon, gone surly and silent. Sexless, that's what they were. She stood letting her mind open to darkness, to forces now moving across Ere, powers that excited her and made her blood pound. Forces she understood and could draw to this place.

She *would* have the bell. She *would* call forth a child to join the stone. And she would shape both child and stone to darkness.

Then Ere would kneel to her will. Then the entire land would be her courtyard and all men her willing servants. And the Seers—the Carriolinian Seers—would be as docile to her as the horses of Eresu had been to RilkenDal.

And the gods, Kish? And the sacred valley of Eresu? What of them?

There were no such things as gods, no such place as Eresu. Urdd, yes. Urdd was real and flaming and violent with the anger of the earth ripping it. Urdd was alive and cruel and satisfying.

But Eresu with its Luff'Eresi was simply a dream without substance, the crutch of weak men afraid to live on their own terms.

She left the tethered, dying mare, and stood staring up at the flying lizards, then reached out with a cold power and laid a cloud over their dim minds that made them wobble in flight and begin to circle uncertainly. She made one come down so close to the tethered mare that the imbecilic animal threw herself futilely against her tether. Kish smiled. Yes, she could tame the lizards, dumb and nasty-tempered as they were. She let the creature return to its friends. She found the path Dracvadrig had worn smooth with his hard, scaly body over years of use and started down. It was just dusk.

By dawn she was standing outside the locked gate, watching the two within with cold distaste. Idiots. Sleeping as far apart as they could in the wide cave. She watched the girl stir, then wake, and Kish drew back into the shadow of the cliff, blocking. Perhaps the girl would go to the boy now, touch him. But no, she knelt beside the dark wolf and began to dress his wounds. Stupid child! The two were as dense and sexless as any humans she had ever encountered.

They must breed! What else was there to do, male and female alone! What else, when her curses tied them so strongly!

At last she fetched food from the ogres' cave and set it inside the bars, then left them, sick at the sight of them. She would not let them starve, though. That was not part of her plan.

Lobon woke, sensed her approach, watched her come to the bars and shove the bowl inside. He did not move. The sense of her was always around them, growing stronger or weaker as she moved about the abyss, suffocating them when she stood close, tolerable only when she was above in the valley.

He and Meatha could speak to the mare up there, but the poor creature was so miserable and sick she had ceased to say much, so weak from mistreatment, from lack of enough food that they were not sure she would live. Even Michennann was able to do little for her except to bring mouthfuls of green grass when the warrior queen had gone.

Lobon watched Meatha kneeling in the gray dawn, tending Feldyn, her dark hair tumbled over one shoulder, the pale skin of her neck like silk against the wolf's dark coat as she leaned to lay her cheek against his head. He rose from his stone bed. The gash across his shoulder was stiff and sore, not healing properly, for they had no healing herbs. Meatha looked across at him. "We need birdmoss. For you. For Feldyn." She said nothing about her own burns. "Michennann could bring birdmoss, carry a little in her mouth. Somewhere where the valleys are green there will be birdmoss beside a running stream. . . ."

"It will do little good to be healed if the sick mare dies and there is only one mount to carry us out. Michennann had best stay with her. It's a slow business, carrying grass. . . ."

"It's no good to have a mount, Lobon, if you're dead of festering wounds!" Kneeling, her hand on Feldyn's shoulder, she spoke out in silence to Michennann, ignoring Lobon's advice.

When she raised her head at last, she Saw the gray mare in sharp vision rising into the morning sky, flying swiftly beside the black cliff, saw her rise to keep clear of the bad-tempered lizards. "She will bring birdmoss," she said, glancing at Lobon. He looked back at her. He guessed she was right. He knew she was beautiful. His need of her began again to run wild; he turned and moved away from her deeper into the cave. "Bring water," she called after him, her own voice tight with restraint.

He filled the waterskin, which Kish had inexplicably returned to them. But what else would Kish do? She could not breed a son from would-be lovers who were dying of thirst. Or maybe she thought that, with less time spent carrying water in cupped hands, there would be more time for idleness, and so for desire. He returned and knelt beside Feldyn, to tip the waterskin to the wolf's mouth. Meatha moved away at once. *As Seers need, so Seers cleave, and in cleaving bring new life.* The heat of Kish's curse never abated.

They ate at last from the bowl Kish had left, sharing the mass of boiled roots and reptiles equally with the wolves. The wolves thought it delicious. It made Meatha and Lobon retch. Feldyn licked the bowl clean.

"When Feldyn is healed," Meatha said, "we must go from this place. We cannot—" She looked at him pleadingly. "We cannot stay here together."

He stared at the locked gate.

"Could we—go deeper into the cave?" she asked. "Could there be another way out? I can—sometimes I think I can feel something there. Not very clearly, but does something call to us from deeper in?"

He looked at her, tried to answer, and found himself reaching for her. She rose and moved away.

"*You* could go," he said, deflated and miserable. "If I could make Kish open the gate, if I could trick her, you could call Michennann down, you. . . ."

"Trick her how? And where would I go? Except—except to find the seventh stone."

He frowned at her, puzzled. "The seventh stone?"

"Kish carries six. If we—"

"She carries the stone that was Dracvadrig's. The two you took from Carriol. And three that were Ramad's. But the seventh stone is here." He held the wolf bell out to her. "Inside the belly of the wolf."

Meatha stared, and she reached to touch the rearing bronze wolf; but at once she drew her hand back.

"I thought you knew," he said. "The dark seems unable to touch it. The power of the wolves—or maybe Skeelie's power reaching. . . ."

"Skeelie? Skeelie of Carriol?"

"She is—Skeelie is my mother. My father was Ramad," he said simply.

It was moments before she spoke. He could feel her confusion, and her sharp interest. When she did speak, her voice was barely audible. "Ramad—Ramad lived generations ago." But her eyes were wide as she considered the truth. "Ramad —did move through Time," she whispered. "How—how *can* such a thing be?"

He tried to give her a sense of Ramad's life, the same sense, the same scenes that Skeelie had given him so often, Time warping and thrusting Ram forward into generations not yet born in his time. And as Lobon wrapped her in the visions of Ramad's life, a change swept Lobon himself, twisted his very soul, the final changing sense of what Ramad was, what Ramad's life had meant.

And so what his own life meant.

She sat Seeing it all, sensing with him the power of Ramad's quest for the shards of the runestone, gripped by Ramad's commitment, by the urgency that Ramad had felt, even in his own time, for the salvation of Ere.

When the vision faded, she sat silent. He could not remember having moved so close to her. It was impossible to keep from touching her. Now she shared Ramad's life with him, shared his memory with him. When he took her hand, she startled; but she rose and moved away. Then she turned a forbidding look back at him that only made his desire stronger. He stood up, meaning to go to her, but a stir of wind at the bars made him turn back. Michennann was there, her wings flared against the sky. As she thrust her soft gray nose between the bars, Meatha ran to her, then hugged her through the bars and wept against the mare's cheek as Michennann nuzzled her.

At last Michennann drew back, placed her muzzle in Meatha's outstretched hands, and spit a great wad of birdmoss into her palms, shaking her nose afterward at the sharp bitter taste. She nuzzled Meatha's cheek once more, then she was gone, in a lifting hush of wings, almost straight up through the abyss. They could feel her terror of the abyss, her repulsion. Meatha watched her out of sight, then turned to dressing Feldyn's wound with a little of the birdmoss.

When Feldyn was comfortable, she made Lobon lie down, and bared and dressed his shoulder. The birdmoss was still damp from the stream. He watched her, and he wanted to hold her.

"We must not," she said coldly. She tied the bandage and left him, rubbing the birdmoss from her hands into the burns that scarred her arms. The remaining moss she laid on a stone.

His passion remained like a fever, he could not turn his mind from her. His dreams of her soared and swept him away so he woke exhilarated and needing, then woke fully to feel only frustration. He knew his passion was of Kish's making, that its results if ever it were let free, would threaten all of Ere, but still he was miserable. He did not know what Meatha dreamed, though at times her desire reached burning to him.

And Meatha began to think privately, If we bred a child, a child that could be hidden safe from Kish and from the dark forces, a child to wield the stone long after we are dead, a child—Lobon's child . . . a child who would keep safe the forces of light. . . .

She began to waver in her resolve. She wanted Lobon, she wanted to be one with him. She turned away from him again and again, biting back tears.

"Meatha?"

She could not look at him directly. Her hands shook. His presence, his powers, drew her like a creature in a snare. He moved toward her.

Feldyn growled. Crieba stepped between them, snarling.

He dropped his hand and stepped back. He stared down at Crieba's cold eyes, and sense returned to him. "I will try to find a way out," he said flatly. "A way back through the cave." And he left them.

WELL BEFORE DAWN, Michennann spoke silently but so urgently that Meatha jerked upright. She thought the mare was again at the gate, but saw only emptiness beyond the bars. *Cammett has died. She is lying twisted in the traces that bound her. But her spirit is free now, free.* Meatha understood then that Michennann spoke from the valley above. The mare's terrible sadness tore at her, Michennann's terrible hatred of the warrior queen.

When she looked up and saw that Lobon was not in the cave, it took her a minute to remember that he was not simply getting a drink of water. Had he found a way out? Oh, he would not go without her. She felt a moment of panic, and then she reached out to him, searching, afraid to hope that there was another entrance to this cave. How could there be? The dragon would never have locked them here if they could escape.

She felt his presence, as warm and close as if he knelt beside her; Saw his face in a sudden vision and had to smile, so smeared with dirt was he, his cheeks and nose, his hands —his hands were bleeding, the nails torn where he clutched a stone. He had been digging in the cave wall. As she watched, he thrust his arm through the small hole he had made, she felt him reach into empty space, sensed now the narrow tunnel beyond. *It was blocked,* he told her, *a wall of dirt and stone. And the earth charred as if the fire ogres had built it. Come Meatha, quickly. Help Feldyn if you can while I dig it out so we can get through.*

She wrapped the wolves' chains around their necks as best she could. Crieba pushed ahead. Feldyn came slowly, hobbling, caught in the pain of his wounds. She could sense Lobon's tension, was linked with Lobon and the wolves in careful blocking to prevent discovery by the warrior queen.

Meatha and the wolves were soon past the trickle of water in the inner tunnel, could hear Lobon digging now. Then suddenly they felt Kish's presence somewhere out in the abyss. They pushed on faster, Feldyn ignoring his pain. The dark wolf pressed against her to hurry her. Then Kish was at the gate, they could hear her opening it. They felt her alarm, then her sharp, angry cry echoed down the tunnel. "Gone! They are gone! Bring swords, bring—hurry, you stupid beasts!"

They sensed her searching the cave, then pushing deeper in, sensed fire ogres shuffling behind her covering the ground too quickly. Soon behind them the tunnel began to grow red, and they knew that the ogres had pushed past Kish in their predatory and mindless quest.

They came on Lobon suddenly, pulling rocks away from a small ragged hole in the stone and earthen walls. He pushed Meatha through, Crieba leaped after her, then Lobon lifted Feldyn, for the dark wolf could not jump. Meatha took Feldyn's shoulders, heavy as lead, and at last they got him through. He stood on unsteady legs, then moved ahead again as the fiery light behind them increased.

They hurried, pressed against one another in the narrow space. Soon behind them they heard rock being torn away from the hole, heard the bulky ogres pushing through. Lobon picked Feldyn up, and they ran. But the dark wolf weighed heavy, Meatha could feel Lobon tire, feel the throbbing pain in his shoulder and arm. "Let me take part of his weight," she whispered. Feldyn snarled in protest, then was still.

With Feldyn's forelegs on Meatha's shoulders and Lobon carrying his rear, they moved faster though clumsily in what, in other circumstances, would have been a ludicrous scene, but was now too desperate to be funny. And even with their increased speed, Kish and the ogres were gaining. At another turning in the tunnel, when fire flared close behind, Feldyn leaped free in spite of his hurt leg and stood beside Crieba facing the advancing fire ogres. Kish pushed forward between them, her bow taut. "You will go no farther . . . ." But the wolves leaped and tore at her so she dropped her bow; her knife flashed; Lobon struck an ogre with a rock, struck again, was past it and on the warrior queen as she slashed at Crieba; it was then they saw the fissure, a small crevice in the rock that seemed to go some distance. Lobon's thought flashed at Meatha. *Get in there! Take Feldyn! It's too small for ogres!* More fire ogres were pushing up the tunnel from the cave. Meatha balked. Lobon grabbed her and pushed her into the crevice as Crieba leaped at Kish.

"I won't leave you, I—"

"Take Feldyn, he—" And Lobon twisted away to face the warrior queen and ogres. Feldyn snarled at Meatha and pushed her into the crevice, crowded in after her, pressing her on. Behind them the battle was fierce.

When she paused, Feldyn snarled and leaped at her. She went on at last, kept pushing in, the space so tight in places she had to squeeze. She could feel Feldyn's pain sharply as he pushed through. The sounds of battle echoed behind them; then suddenly there was the sound of falling rocks. What had happened? She could make no picture come. Ahead she saw flame and thought fire ogres were there too, then saw it was molten lava far below, that they had come through the tunnel to a ledge high along the side of a cavern. Where was Lobon? What was happening?

At last Crieba appeared, and Lobon behind him; and she went weak with relief.

"The tunnel was filled with ogres," he panted.

"That noise, like falling rocks . . . ?"

"I pulled boulders down to block the tunnel. There were too many, we couldn't fight them." She felt his shame at having fled. She touched his cheek, and he put his arms around her. They clung together, let their need for solace take them for a moment, her face pressed into the leather of his tunic, the wolf bell hurting her ribs; and suddenly they were caught in a vision of a city on fire, men battling among burning buildings, then of winged ones above leaping through red smoky sky—winged ones carrying dark riders, Kubalese riders; then the winged ones began deliberately to fall, smashing to earth, their riders under them. They Saw for an instant the whole of Ere torn with warring; then Meatha pulled away from Lobon, ceased to touch the bell, and the vision was gone. He let out his breath.

"They were fighting on the border of Carriol," he said with fury. "Carriol's armies are driven back to the border." He had never cared, before, about Carriol. Not as he now cared.

They found a way leading downward, and only when they reached the floor of the cavern did they stop to rest. They could sense nothing following them. The air seemed fresher to their left, and they saw an opening in the far wall. They crossed to it, ducked low beneath stone, then stood staring upward with drawn breath.

Far above them in the roof of the cavern shone a jagged hole with a patch of sky beyond, sky gray with storm. As they watched, clouds blew across swept by fast winds. "There was a hole like that in another cavern," Meatha said, "where I first met Anchorstar." But this opening was so very distant.

To their right a crude stairway was cut into the wall, wide steps as if made for the use of fire ogres. They crossed to it and began to climb. The steps were scorched by ogre's feet. The sounds of their footsteps made a scuffing echo across the cavern. They sensed that somewhere above them their ascent was noted, and awaited.

Then suddenly the wolves stiffened and began to stalk, and from around the bend ahead three fire ogres came shuffling, creatures awash with red flame. Lobon held the wolf bell high, and his power joined with the wolves—unfettered now by Kish's answering power—to drive the creatures stumbling backward up the steps until they turned at last and shuffled into a high crevice. Surely they were more docile than the other fire ogres. Was it because of the bell's power? Or was their little group together growing stronger?

Or perhaps these creatures were more used to humans and not so easily nudged to fury. Did men come here, then? And why?

They knew before they reached the top of the cavern that winged ones waited there, tied in small cells. Yes, men had been here. Dark Seers. For these were RilkenDal's fettered mounts, captive and beaten and starving. They were of the bands from the far mountains that had been so long silent, they whose brothers were at this moment killing themselves deliberately in battle, to turn the outcome of the wars. Twenty winged horses waited, all of them scarred and stiff with wounds, burned from the fire ogre's touch, their wings bound with leather cords, their heads tied to bolts in the stone.

When they reached them, Meatha and Lobon went sick at the sight of them. The horses were so thin and weak. They came away from their bonds walking stiffly, trying to lift wings grown heavy with disuse. Meatha's hand shook as she began to dress wounds with the little birdmoss that was left. She applied the moss as tenderly as she could into the long gash on a white mare's chest, wincing as the mare flinched with pain. She tore up the rest of her shift for bandages.

For four days they camped on the ledge high up the wall of the cavern. Lobon found grain in a cavern below, kept there by RilkenDal for the horses he took into battle. They found charred leather buckets by a water runlet and carried them countless times up to the winged ones.

From this height they could see lakes of fire strung across the cave floor below like a necklace. Above, through the high opening that was still so far away, they watched the first night as the sky darkened; then they crouched in the stalls away from the storm that broke with a terrible violence, drenching the cave. When at last the sky cleared and the sun shone weakly, the wind, twisting down into the cavern, was bitterly cold.

There was a constant but gentler wind, too, of beating wings, as the horses of Eresu worked at strengthening unused muscles so they could fly once more. Soon some of the horses began to descend to the floor of the cavern to drink, though they did not like going there. When the earth began again to tremble, they became nervous and would startle and sweep up into the heights of the cavern without drinking. Then on the third night a gusher of lava broke out of the cave wall below them and flowed in a river toward the molten lakes.

As the lava spilled onto the floor, fire ogres began to appear from fissures in the cave below and to move ponderously toward the lava river, then to shuffle along and around it in a cumbersome and terrifying ritual. A few turned away and came up the stairs toward the ledge, but two winged stallions rose and struck at them from the air with sharp hooves until the clumsy creatures fell to the floor below. The wolves killed a third with quick, striking slashes, then lay licking their burns. Lobon killed two with a rock and sent another over the side by tripping it. The flaming, twisting bodies lit the cave walls as they fell.

When the last ogre was gone, Meatha curled at once into the hollow of stone where she slept, trying to get warm. Crieba came to lie beside her, and she wished it were Lobon there. But when she caught his unspoken words and saw him watching her, she made a wall between them until he lay down at last beside a winged stallion to shelter from the wind that blew down on them in sharp gusts.

When Lobon woke, the wind was still. Moonlight touched the cavern from above; and the mountain was trembling in long violent rumbles; that was what had waked him. All around him winged ones were up, balancing with open wings, for the ledge had become a turmoil of moving rock. Meatha clung to a dark stallion; the white mare pushed close to Lobon crying, *Mount, Lobon! Mount!* The shocks were violent, wave upon wave. The cave could shift or collapse, they could be trapped here. Lobon grabbed Feldyn and lifted him between the mare's wings, and she leaped toward the hole above. He got Crieba mounted, felt the wolf's fear. "Hang on with your teeth! Crouch between her wings and hang on!" He saw Meatha mounted and flung himself onto a pale stallion, grabbed a handful of mane, and felt the world drop away from him as he was swept away; felt wings fold tight around him as the stallion slipped through the hole; felt drowned by wind as the stallion beat his way out onto the open sky to make way for those coming behind.

They were free of the cave. Free. But they stood on unsteady, trembling ground; and then suddenly they were caught in a confusion of battle come out of nowhere, out of the sky all around them, no hint, no sense of it beforehand. Heavy wings beat at them, sharp-toothed lizards tore at them, diving, then wheeling away. Lobon had no weapon. The stallion he rode struck and bit. The sky was filled with lizards. Winged horses screamed. Lobon tried to see Meatha, felt teeth tear his arm. The sound of beating wings, of screams, of the earth thundering, all were mixed and confused. The stallion struck and struck, and soon below Lobon could see a dark smear of bodies on the moonwashed earth. Lizards? Horses of Eresu? Where were Feldyn, Crieba? Meatha's command was sharp. *The wolf bell, Lobon! Use the power you carry!*

But he had no chance, for the lizards were drawing way. Almost as quickly as they had come, they were gone, a stutter of wings then a black flock like huge birds against the moon-washed sky.

Why? What had called them away?

The stallion came to earth. Lobon slid down. The dark stallion who carried Meatha winged to earth and she slipped down, to rest her head against the horse's withers. Ere's two moons hung like half-closed eyes in an empty sky. Lobon stared at Meatha.

"Why did they leave? It was Kish guiding them. Why would she call them off?"

"She never meant for them to attack," she said with certainty. "They—can't you feel it? She can hardly control them. She meant only to follow us. She has sensed something —something . . . ." She frowned, groping to put vague images together. "She has sensed something—that I have sensed, Lobon." She was trembling with the need to See more clearly. What was it? So close, so urgent yet so hard to See. "Something that has lain in my thoughts. Something Anchor-star knew," she whispered. "Kish senses it." She turned to look away in the direction the lizards had disappeared. "Kish means to follow us, Lobon. She thinks we will seek—that we. . . ." she caught her breath ". . . that we know where the eighth stone lies!"

They stared at one another. Slowly, frowning, she began to pull knowledge out of the deeper reaches of her mind, reaches touched by Anchorstar. Slowly a vision began to unfold, the vision Anchorstar had given her: a green valley and the crystal dome. A white-haired child. And, as if she had forgotten half the vision, a sense of power now couched beneath the crystal dome: power that could be only one thing.

"A stone lies there," she whispered.

"Yes." He Saw the vision as clearly as she. The wolves Saw it. A shard of the runestone beneath a crystal dome in the center of a bright green valley.

"Kish sees it, too," Meatha said.

"She means to follow. She means to see us find the stone, and then . . . then. . . ."

She reddened, swallowed. "Then see our child born. Take the stones and our child." She felt a stab of pain as if, indeed, there were a child, tender and helpless. A child so very vital to Ere. And now she felt pain and shame at having taken the stones from Carriol, pain at her self-deception. And she saw in Lobon's eyes the knowledge of his own self-deception. She felt his shame at having so long ignored the truth of what he must do, and what his life must mean.

She touched his shoulder. He put his arms around her, rested his brow against her hair, and they knew as one the blind, twisted paths they had both followed, so willful, so dangerous for Ere. Something of their spirits joined in that moment that could never again be parted.

Something much dearer, much stronger than Kish could ever create with her spells.

At last they stepped apart without speaking.

Crieba had gone to hunt. Feldyn watched them drowsily as they gathered sticks for firewood among the sparse low bushes. The winged ones were scattered across the rounded butt of mountain, grazing the thick grass greedily. There were no trees for shelter here, only stunted brush. The mountain was ancient, long ago worn nearly flat—though still it rose higher than the surrounding peaks. Only two peaks, to the south, were higher. Eken-dep with her glacier, and the peak that both were sure was Tala-charen, for still a power like a voice reached out to them from that conelike mountain.

When the fire was burning well, Meatha went to stand alone where the mountain dropped off into space.

How were they to find the crystal dome? In what place lay the green valley? She had had no sense of its direction. And if they found it, could they avoid leading the warrior queen there?

And how were they to get the six stones that Kish herself possessed?

Quietly, with all the strength she could muster, she reached out to Tala-charen and tried to draw its power into herself. But no strength touched her; she could not make herself feel stronger. In desperation she reached beyond Tala-charen to Carriol, for she needed Anchorstar now; he must speak to her.

But she could get no sense of him. She stood vainly trying for some minutes, then suddenly, sharply, she Saw the white-haired child. *Jaspen*. Her name was Jaspen. She Saw the stone itself then. A long shard of jade lying in the child's curled hand.

But where? Where was the crystal dome? Where dwelt Jaspen?

When nothing more came, she turned away, swallowing. Never once had there been a sense of Anchorstar. Only the disembodied vision. She went slowly back to the fire and sat down close to Feldyn, seeking the wolf's strength, seeking comfort. Feldyn laid his head in her lap. She leaned over him, stroked his cheek, then leaned her forehead against his, trying not to cry. The stone in the vision seemed so close. But where? Where?

Chapter
Ten

LOBON WOKE to bright moonlight and to the howl of wolves. He sat up, could see Feldyn and Crieba beyond the camp, silhouetted against moon-silvered clouds, gazing off toward the southeast. He tried to sense what they sensed and could not. They raised their muzzles again in wails that shattered the night. Meatha woke and came closer to the fire. The winged ones stirred, lifted their heads in alarm, spread their wings ready for flight; then at the wolves' reassurance, they settled down once more. Lobon scowled. What was this all about? But already the two wolves were returning. Feldyn nuzzled him and took his arm between sharp teeth as he was wont to do when he was in high spirits. *Our brothers speak to us, Lobon, our brothers descended from Fawdref. We feel more than their strength now, we hear their voices clearly.* Feldyn stretched and gazed again toward Carriol. *They battle the Kubalese now alongside Carriol's warriors, to defend the border of Carriol.* The wolf's golden eyes were filled with intense and mysterious promise. *Wolves of our pack battle the dark, Lobon. And they speak to Crieba and me. They know the crystal dome, where lies a shard of the runestone. They know the vision Meatha carries.*

Meatha caught her breath. "Can they show us?" But already she, like Lobon, was being pulled into the vision of the small green valley with its crystal dome; but now they Saw it from a wider vantage, Saw it was surrounded by dunes and by vast reaches of sand. "The high desert," Meatha breathed. And behind the valley on one side rose a line of mountains, and higher peaks behind these with five sharp peaks marching just beyond a vast sweep of granite, pale in the moonlight. And far behind these, another peak towered higher still, a peak shaped like Tala-charen, though different in some way that Meatha could not make out.

"Different because it's the other side, I think," Lobon said. "As if the crystal dome lies on the far side of Tala-charen, to the north of it—there where the desert must sweep around the end of the Ring of Fire." He raised his eyes to her. "If that is so, then the valley lies far up in the unknown lands."

"But we can find it now, we—"

"We have only to move across the skies above Tala-charen until we see that great slab of granite." He rose, pulled on his boots. He did not mean to wait until morning.

"Kish will follow us," she said.

"I hope so. She carries the stones—I don't want her far away." Though he felt naked without a weapon, though he would have sold his soul for sword or bow.

They made ready at once. Lobon lifted the wolves onto the backs of two winged mares; Meatha mounted, then Lobon; and they were leaping skyward into the moon-silvered night, flying light and fast across a cold quick wind. To their left rose Eken-dep, its white glacier touched by moonlight; then suddenly against that mass of white a small, dark silhouette appeared in the sky, moving fast toward them. Kish? All of them startled.

But Kish would not come alone now that she had lizards to fight beside her.

Then they saw it was not a lizard but a winged one coming on fast and riderless, flying free. Michennann, cutting the wind in great sweeps of her wings, coming at last to join them.

But now behind Michennann, peppering the sky, the lizards appeared beating across the face of the glacier. The sense of Kish came predatory and cold. The winged horses needed no urging, they fled above the wild peaks; and the lizards followed, settling into a steady pace, but never drawing closer. Michennann winged near to the white mare who carried Meatha. How scarred she was from battling the lizards. There was a welt across her neck and down her side, and her silver coat was torn with deep scratches. But the sense of her spirit was warm and close, and all enmity between them was now gone and only sympathy remained.

When at last they drew near to Tala-charen, Meatha could feel its power—and feel Lobon's quickening interest. The dark stallion Lannthenn, who carried him, swept close to the peak and the others followed, hovering so close for a few moments that wingtips nearly touched the cave entrance, and they could see into the cave where Ramad had stood. Meatha shuddered with the power of the place. Here the runestone had split; here Seers had come suddenly out of Time to receive the broken shards.

The cave floor was translucent green like the sea. They all thought how that floor had split, the very mountain split to swallow the bones of the gantroed, then had closed up once more. They thought of Ram and Skeelie there, two young children caught in a clashing of powers that shook all of Ere —that changed all of Ere—and that had brought them here this night on a quest to undo that splitting. It was impossible not to think of the Luff'Eresi, impossible not to think of them as gods, and wonder as men had wondered for generations whether it had been they who had placed the stone in this cave; and whether their powers had touched the stone the night of the splitting.

Then the winged ones banked and swept away, leaving Tala-charen behind.

Beyond Tala-charen they began to hear rumbles from the land below, and twice they saw explosions of fire in the mountains far to the north. They were flying over mountains still, but now the desert lay ahead, a white smear against the sky; and soon they saw the foot of the peaks had begun to curve northward skirting the vast white dunes. It was not long afterward that they saw the pale granite cliff tilting to the sky. Then they were over the white dunes, gleaming like snow below them. They began to stare downward between the horses' beating wings, searching among the closer dunes for the small green valley. Behind them, the lizards paced them, never varying their distance; and Kish watched them.

To the north among the mountains, red smoke rose into the moon-pale clouds. Flame belched from a far peak, then was still. They could hear earthshocks, some of them faint as a whisper. All eyes searched the dunes below, searched the black half-moons of shadow deep between dunes, for the valley and for the gleam of the crystal dome. And they could feel and sense more than earthshocks around them, for other powers were gathering, too: Powers awakened by the dark Seers, and powers nurtured by the light. Both powers were alerted and building, clashing crosswise against one another, powers that drew strength from that very clashing. Drew strength from the rising need of the Seers and the desire to control the fate of the stones. For the stones were like a magnet now to all the forces that rose across Ere. The forces of good swelled and drew in around the little flying band, and the powers of dark drew around the warrior queen, whose evil was older than Time. And the powers, by drawing close, strengthened yet again—just as, below the flying bands, the powers of the earth itself broke into new fissures as the earth cracked, and so built to crescendo.

Along the coastal countries, shocks came so harsh they brought down houses and outbuildings. Fissures opened across the fields, and terrified animals stampeded. A ewe with a lamb ran blindly into a crack opening a hundred feet deep. The river Urobb flooded its banks just above Sangur and drowned a small village in its sweeping tide. The bloodthirsty Herebians, many of them wounded and beaten by Carriol, backed off from warring and thought of returning home—but only to wait for the holocaust that seemed imminent and that would give them sure victory. For well they remembered past upheavals. Always, the Herebians had risen first and strongest after the wild heaving of the land. Always, the Herebians had taken the spoils as other men cowered in fear before volcanoes they thought were the gods' wrath.

Kearb-Mattus gathered his scattered forces. He did not let them draw away to wait out the holocaust as they wished, but sent them riding hard toward Carriol's border, for what better time to destroy Carriol than when accompanied by the violence of the land itself. And while his main band rode toward Carriol, Kearb-Mattus himself with fifty troops rode hard for Farr, where his scouts told him Kish's cults marched, led by the adolescent Carriolinian upstarts. So they thought to help defend the border of Carriol! He had not known until an hour before that they had had the nerve to fetter those among them who held to the ways of Kubal and to Kish, and to lock them into the old villa at Dal and bar the portals with stone and mortar. Brash, snivelling . . . Kearb-Mattus smiled and thought with heat of killing the two young Seers who led that crew. He knew them. Oh, how he would pleasure himself by their deaths, those two that had so defied him—fracking brats—before he took Burgdeeth two years ago. Those two that had destroyed the training of the Children of Ynell there in the drug-caves of Kubal. They would die now, and painfully.

LOBON SAW THE EMERALD VALLEY FIRST, hidden in a moon-shaped crease between dunes, visible only because the crystal dome reflected moonlight. They could not have missed it in any case, however, for a sense of power had begun to draw them, the sense of the runestone there. They feared for that runestone now, for Kish was close behind. Lobon turned to look back at her. Her lizards were massing close around her, as if for attack. But still she kept her distance. Lobon leaned between the dark stallion's wings as he swept down over the valley, a shadowed niche now between the silvered dunes. The dome glinted, then lost itself as their angle of descent steepened, then gleamed again; once it reflected Ere's moons just before they came to earth.

They came down onto heavy grass. The winged ones folded their wings along their backs and stood facing the crystal dome. Behind and above them, Kish's band drew close, sweeping over and back. Lobon could feel power strong now from the stone that dwelt beneath the dome. How had it come here? How had the dome come here? And who was the white-haired child? He did not dismount from Lannthenn's back, nor did Meatha dismount. She looked across at him in silence. Her fear and her exhilaration shook him. They could feel the powers gathered around them, could feel the earth's trembling, could feel the intolerable weight of Ere's very existence balanced in this moment.

Inside the crystal dome, the white-haired child paused, then came slowly to the crystal door and pushed it open.

She came up to Lannthenn's side, carrying a sheathed sword, the sight of which made Lobon start. She wore a second sword. And she held her right fist clenched against her chest. She was tiny, surely no more than seven. Her hair was snow white in the moonlight, her thin shift hardly enough to keep off the cold, though she was not shivering. Her eyes looked, in the moonlight, as golden as a wolf's eyes. *As golden as Anchorstar's eyes,* Meatha told him. With effort the child lifted the sword. Lobon stared again at the hilt, felt weak and strange, took it from her and unsheathed it, sat holding Skeelie's sword. How had it gotten here? "Where is she?" he whispered, glancing past the child into the dome, but he could see no figure there, caught no sense of her.

"Skeelie, your mother, bids you take her sword," was all the child would say. "The silver sword that Ramad forged for her." Then she held up her partly closed fist to him and without another word, without any hesitation, she laid the heavy jade in his hand.

It was surely the largest of all the shards; a heavy, thick dagger of jade nearly as long as his palm, carved with the runes that were its own fragment of the whole rune:

power   end   life

Lobon held it for a moment then slipped it into the inner lining of his tunic beside the wolf bell. He watched the two wolves leap clear of the winged horses that had carried them. They went directly to the child and stood head-high beside her, facing toward the warrior queen sweeping and wheeling in the sky above.

Lobon knew he must carry the stone into battle. They all knew, as if the child had told them, that Kish could not take the runestone from the crystal dome; that this stone was the true lure to draw Kish, and so retrieve the six stones she carried—the bait on which the fate of all eight stones waited.

The child unbuckled the second sword and handed it to Meatha. Then Lobon turned Lannthenn skyward with a thought, the stallion as eager as he to do battle. The white mare wheeled next to him, Meatha taut with nerves, and all the winged ones following, mind meeting mind as they formed a rhythm of attack. Ahead, the winged lizards swarmed, hissing. Kish swept out ahead of the pack, her sword drawn, her power in the stones she carried like a sword itself. The sky had begun to go milky with the coming dawn. Kish's lizards slithered beneath heavy wings in a close-flying swarm as Kish swept down toward Lobon.

AND ACROSS ERE, Kearb-Mattus came in silence down along the Owdneet. He followed Zephy and Thorn and the cultists, formed now into a nearly respectable fighting band.

Zephy and Thorn knew he followed, though the sense of him was garbled, often lost, as if Seers rode with him. Pellian street rabble, and untrained. Their own band moved slowly, for half their troops marched, only half rode, the horses in short supply. All the winged ones were gone, to fight in Carriol. Zephy and Thorn and their companions were exhausted from battling small bands of fighters. They knew they must rest soon, if for only an hour. "Then we must take what troops we can and ride for Carriol," Thorn said, for the battling was desperate there.

No cultists among them now were dissident, for those dissident had already been sealed into the villa at Dal. It had been a battle hardly worth remarking, the awakened cultists seeing at last the true nature of their warrior queen, simply overpowering those who still clung to the ways of Kish, tying them, marching them through Dal to the villa that already Carriolinian soldiers had turned into an outlying prison, and sealing them in with scrap rubble from the sacking of the city that Kearb-Mattus had earlier begun and the heaving of the earth completed.

They had ridden then toward Carriol, through two areas in Farr held still by Carriolinian soldiers, skirted several Kubalese bands in their haste, then across farmland torn by the heaving ground and desolate with wounded and dead, from which the Kubalese had already departed.

KEARB-MATTUS ATTACKED the young Carriolinians as they slept; he was shielded by a mind-blocking held somehow steady by three rude street-Seers, came over a rise onto the handful of mounted men who guarded the camp, and saw the pitiful heap of soldiers beyond sleeping in the open.

Zephy leaped up at the sound of fighting, hardly awake, frightened. Thorn was mounted, shouting at her. She grabbed the bridle of the horse he had brought her and was mounted; all were mounted, weapons ready, the attacking troops everywhere among them so they were hard put not to panic. She lost sight of Thorn, thrust her sword against the belly of a huge Kubalese bearing down on her, ducked beneath his blow to strike again, heard the screams of horses, of men, took a blow across her shoulder, spun her horse around to strike; all was confusion, a melee in the near-dark. She wanted to cry out for Thorn and daren't, felt another blow like fire across her neck, was jerked from her horse, fell, was caught and her arms pulled behind her, then hit again, and she went dizzy and sick.

ALL CARRIOL KNEW that Thorn's band was in trouble—and knew that more Kubalese were on their way toward Carriol's border. Carriol fought for her life, winged ones carried soldiers or fought free without riders, leaping from the sky to strike; the wolves fought as fiercely as they had fought at the battle of Hape and in the dark wood. Only the master Seers remained behind in Carriol, seated in the citadel with heads lowered in the prayer of concentration, massing their power more surely here to help cripple the Kubalese; for though the stone was gone, still some power clung inside the citadel itself, this place that once had known the power of the Luff'Eresi.

IN THE SKY ABOVE the crystal dome, the battle was bloody, a winging whirling melee of winds and confusion. Kish swept her band in again and again to attack the winged ones and Meatha, while Kish herself drove mercilessly at Lobon. And as Kish called on the powers of the creatures of darkness, those spirits reached out to give purpose to the winged lizards: made warring, lethal creatures of them, all claw and teeth and canny in their maneuvering, slashing and twisting away to divert Meatha. The white mare bore streaks of blood across her coat and wings, and Meatha's arm was torn. The warrior queen parried and bore down on Lobon. She slashed, cut Lobon's shoulder, and swept away beneath Lannthenn to come at him from behind with her ready sword. Lannthenn dove and doubled back; Lobon struck, but the warrior queen was away, quick in the air, eluding him. The shuddering earth below rang like death music.

And along Pelli's coast a protrusion of land broke loose and fell into the sea. At the same moment, in Farr, Kearb-Mattus let some of the cultists escape his troops in order to surround and take captive the young Carriolinian Seers; and soon his troops were ushering Zephy and Thorn and five other Seers down from their mounts, to be bound, to be tied one to the other, then to be force-marched off ahead of the horses toward Dal, and toward the villa-turned-cell where they, earlier, had left captives. For that villa, too, had fallen to Kearb-Mattus's men and was now a perfect place to give, with slow, increasing torture, the final death rites the Kubalese leader so anticipated.

Neither Thorn nor Zephy looked up as they marched, nor looked at one another; but their minds were locked as one —angry, desperate—seeking a plan of escape.

LOBON STRUCK a telling blow across Kish's face, another blow that drew blood from the lizard. He saw Meatha skewer a lizard then jerk her sword free as the heavy creature fell. Below them now bodies lay, dark splotches across the meadow and dunes, some lizard, some horses of Eresu, their wings sprawling across the pale sand. Kish was on him again. He parried, forced her back; Kish's lizard clawed air, she gripped its neck, off balance, and he thrust forward quickly —then too late Lobon saw her strategy, too late cried out to Lannthenn and felt the stallion take her sword in a mortal spot.

They were falling, the stallion barely able to keep his wings spread, blood gushing from his torn chest. He was like a crippled bird. Lobon's heart filled with love for him, with sorrow; and with terrible fear for the stones. Lannthenn fell to earth in a twisting, crippled spiral, went to his knees and collapsed as Lobon leaped free.

From the crystal dome Jaspen watched. Feldyn and Crieba stood immobile beside her. She made prayer for Lobon, violent strong prayer—had done so constantly since the battle began.

She was the child of Cadach, the tree man, the youngest child of five, though no two were born in the same generation or in the same place nor, for that, of the same mother; but all born with the spiritual need to atone for the sins of Cadach. And this was her atonement, this guarding of the stone that now, through her giving of it, stood in balance and held all of Ere's fate in balance.

Soon behind her come at the force of her prayer, towering figures made of light rose from the stuff of the crystal dome as if that crystal were but air, figures unclear in their dimension, and their wings all woven of light. They watched the battle, watched Lannthenn fall and die; watched the warrior queen descend to the meadow where Lobon stood awaiting her, holding the stone and the wolf bell as bait.

Kish remained mounted. Around her, lizards came out of the sky to slither in the grass circling Lobon. Above, half a dozen lizards drove Meatha and the white mare back, attacking them again and again.

Kish's mount spun and twisted so she jerked it savagely and brought it rearing over Lobon. He stabbed at its belly, ducked her sword, stabbed again as the creature twisted away; then he leaped and hit it, dodging Kish's blows, forcing his power at her; felt her sword pierce his arm. And he felt a surge of power in himself—as if all the Seers of Carriol sent power flooding like a tide. He struck the lizard, struck again as it reared, slashed its trailing wing; it tried to climb skyward with injured wings, and he struck once more down its side with all his weight on his sword, and it fell screaming. Kish beat it, but it could not rise. She left it to die, slid down, faced Lobon, her face white and twisted with fury and with lust for the stones he carried, her blade gleaming as she raised it. The power of the stones seemed undistinguishable now from the power of the forces that shook Ere. All across Ere the earth heaved; in Carriol the forces of light were driven back by the heaving earth as well as by dark troops.

From the crystal dome, the child Jaspen watched and held her power steady. She felt the power of the two wolves who stood beside her, felt Meatha's power supporting Lobon, as all together they sought to weaken Kish and drive her back.

Cadach the tree man Saw the battle, felt the earth's tremors around him and knew their true nature. Trapped inside his ancient tree deep in the caves of Owdneet, he felt the mountain move above him, below him, Saw the warring in Carriol and Carriol's armies driven back. Then felt the mountain gave way beneath him; his tree toppled suddenly into a newly opened fissure, the roots upside down reached up like clawing fingers as it was swept, with all the treasures of the cave, deep into the center of the world. And Cadach at last knew death, crushed inside the shattered tree.

But the spirit of Cadach was not dead, it came truly alive suddenly and watched all of Ere in the holocaust. Cadach, dead at last and his spirit released, watched Lobon's battle with terrible empathy.

He Saw the crystal dome and knew it stood on the place where once a jade sphere had been mined. He Saw the mining of the jade, Saw that miner-Seer discover the powers of the stone. He Saw its theft by another, the search for it, Saw it all in an instant, Saw finally a procession of Seers carry the stone up into the mountain Tala-charen to safety and leave it for fate and for the natural forces beyond their own will, to deal with.

And so had those forces dealt, and were dealing. Cadach went still in his mind as those forces massed, and as Kish's sword struck across Lobon's, struck again. He Saw Kish take a blow and reel, then strike cruelly at Lobon, Saw the battle in the sky above, where Meatha fought desperately to join him.

From the crystal dome a woman stood looking out past the white-haired child and the two wolves: Skeelie, come out of Time as silent as wings muffled by cloud; Skeelie, held tense now by the force of the battle. Convulsively she moved forward, her eyes never leaving the battle, her hand gripping the heavy, unfamiliar sword at her side, for she carried Canoldir's sword. She pushed through the dome, touched the clear door, would go to Lobon, would fight beside Lobon. . . .

And then as she passed the child and the wolves, she slowed and drew back again, for the warrior queen was weakening. Skeelie brought force strong with the others, felt forces strong around Lobon. She did not know she was whispering Ramad's name, like an incantation. She stood, sword ready but unmoving, as Lobon parried powerfully against Kish, driving her back now, giving her mortal blows in a surge of fury and strength. Kish rallied suddenly, swung her sword with wild angry fear, struck, then stabbed into his chest in a flashing move; metal rang; her sword glanced away.

He did not fall. He staggered, righted himself and drove the warrior queen back. He felt the power of the great wolves, felt power join him strong as a beating pulse, as all across Ere Seers of light turned from their own battles, held their attackers at bay, their powers joined with Lobon in the stones. The warrior queen lunged and slashed, but in her fury she was losing control; she slashed wildly, and he drove her back again, again, and then with one lunging, twisting blow he thrust his sword home into her chest, and she fell.

He stood over her, sword ready, but she made no move to rise. He stood quietly, watching her die.

At last Lobon knelt beside her. He stared at her white, reptilian face, shaped with anger even in death. He reached, removed from her tunic the five shards of the runestone of Eresu. Took up the starfires. He wanted to wipe the scent of Kish from them, polish them clean. Instead he rose and reached to place the stones inside his own tunic. It was then he felt the twisted metal there. He pulled the wolf bell forth.

It was smashed and twisted by Kish's sword. The belly of the bitch-wolf gaped open where the blade had gone in. Inside that cut, gleaming green, lay a shard of the runestone. He turned the smashed wolf bell and spilled the stone into his hand beside the other shards. And at once he was stricken with a force like thunder. He felt heat and a white light burst around the stone so bright it blinded him.

When at last the light died, he remained still, shocked, hypnotized with the force that had gripped him.

In his hand lay not the shards of the runestone now, but a round jade sphere. The whole stone. No mark or line showed where the shards had joined. The runes were carved around its surface, the whole rune—or nearly whole: for a chasm ran along one side of the stone deep into the center, a rough-edged chasm where the missing shard should have been. Inside, he could see the golden heart that had been the starfires. He looked up then, and saw Meatha—and Skeelie stood beside her, the look on her face unfathomable, her dark eyes deep with emotions that shook Lobon's very soul, the sense of Ramad so strong between them, the sense of their closeness.

"It is joined," he said inadequately. He felt heavy and stupid with shock. "How—how could such a thing happen? It is not whole, it is flawed. How . . . ?" He was fighting dizziness, fighting to remain standing.

Skeelie moved to support him, stood tall and strong beside him, holding his shoulders. Her voice shook only slightly. "Perhaps it is flawed just—just as Ere is flawed. Just so—as men's lives are flawed."

"Yes," he said, staring down at the stone.

"Though," she added quietly, "that makes their lives no less magnificent."

He leaned against Skeelie, felt her strength, her gentleness. Then he looked across to Meatha, reached to take her hand.

"It is done," Meatha said. Above them the sky was empty, for the remaining lizards had fled.

"And the wolves?" he said suddenly, looking around; for the white-haired child stood alone, a little way from them.

"They are gone," Meatha said. "They make for Carriol and their brothers." He glimpsed them in the shadows of his mind racing across the sand. "They will return to us," she said. "Maybe—maybe with mates by their sides." She smiled. "Too long alone, those two." Her warmth and her strength, like Skeelie's strength, reached out and steadied him; and Skeelie moved away at a little distance.

He looked long at Meatha. "And—are you too long alone?"

She lowered her eyes, then looked up. "I—I am not alone," she said boldly. Kish's spell had fallen from them, and the force that linked them now was their own, not woven of darkness nor of another's greed. He put his arm around her and found the lack of a spell made little difference in the way he felt. He drew her close, then winced as he pressed her against a sword wound. Suddenly he felt the pain of all his wounds, as if the numbing strain of battle had worn away and his senses come clear once again; pain, and then dizziness once more.

He woke with strong hands lifting him to a sitting position, and found himself in a bed, staring dumbly at a steaming mug of something vile. He looked up at Skeelie's face.

"I can't drink that. It stinks."

"Ram always drank it. So can you. It will ease the pain."

He pushed it away. "I don't need droughts for pain." Though pain was nearly crushing him.

Then he began to remember, and the memory so shook him that it too brought pain. He gripped the stone in his hand and dared not look at it.

"Drink!" Skeelie insisted, and he gulped the hot, bitter brew. Not till it was gone did he lift the stone, and read the runes carved into it;

> Eternal quest to those ———— power
> Some seek dark; they ———— end.
> Some hold joy: they know eternal life.
> Through them all powers will sing.

And the child Jaspen, standing silently beside the bed— which surely must be her bed, a narrow cot—said softly, "Eternal quest to those with power. Some seek dark, they mortal end." The touch of the stone seemed like fire to Lobon, the power of it immense, so it filled the light-washed dome. He remembered the moment of the joining, the white light. The stone had joined in his hand just as, six generations gone in Time, it had shattered in Ramad's hand.

On the floor beside the cot lay the split and battered wolf bell. The bitch wolf was still grinning.

The drug was beginning to take hold, to make him muzzy. He remembered the battling across Ere, Carriol's desperate warring against the Kubalese, felt with dulled senses how the powers had struck across Ere, powers of darkness rising—then, sleepily, he realized that the sense of those powers was gone; that a sense of infinite calm lay around him, and lay too across Ere.

He looked up with hazy vision now to see both Meatha and Skeelie watching him, and the child Jaspen standing quietly, her thin little face very calm beneath that shock of white hair.

"The dark is gone," Meatha said. "Or—the dark has drawn back," she corrected herself.

Skeelie touched his cheek. "Perhaps the dark will never be gone entirely. Maybe that is what the flawed stone tells us."

"As long as we are mortal," the child Jaspen said sadly, "the dark will always be somewhere close to us. Even when we are at peace."

"But the land is quiet now," Meatha said. "And the land is different, Lobon. Can you sense it? The land is split apart. When the stone joined, the rift began. The mountains—" she stopped speaking. The vision came around them, flowing from one mind to the other, for all three had Seen it at the moment of the splitting, only Lobon unaware, as if he stood in the blind eye of a storm. They had Seen the fissure begin as a crack high up inside the Ring of Fire, and run jagged and increasing in size, down through the mountains, to cut back and forth across Cloffi and across the river Owdneet, so the river's waters mixed with lava, sending up blinding steam. The rift shouldered south through Aybil, toward Farr and toward the villa of Dal.

SKEELIE AND THORN had sensed it, as had the five young Seers locked with them in the villa at Dal, sensed the rift and cried out with all the power left in them, felt the earth heave and knew that they could die there, Zephy and Thorn clutching one another's wrists in an agony of terror each for the other, and in an agony of power as they sought out for help. They dug at the stone wall, forced their shoulders and backs against the rubble with which their cell was sealed, staring skyward again and again through the small hole they had made, hoping. . . . They felt the earth shift beneath them, they sensed the rift tearing apart the land; and they tore and tore at the wall.

Zephy saw the winged ones first high in the sky above them and cried out. They tore at the stone with bloody hands. Then the sky outside was filled with wings; but they could not get out. *Get back!* the silent voices cried. *Get back!* And winged ones turned their backsides to the wall and kicked, kicked again in a wild drumbeat until at last the wall gave way. Rubble fell around their feet as the earth's heaving increased. The Seers tumbled through, leaped to mount, and the horses swept skyward as the rift below dropped Dal's villa into a fiery maw and crushed and toppled it a hundred feet into the earth. Then the rift went on, hungering for the sea.

The rift shattered through Farr and split the coastal shelf and then the sea floor, and sent the sea leaping out onto the land. Behind it the eleven countries of Ere, so long joined in their isolation from the rest of the primitive globe, were no longer joined. Now to the west lay Moramia and Karra in the high desert, nearly untouched, and clinging to them, Zandour and Aybil and Cloffi. That land was separated now from the eastern nations by the rift half a mile wide, so in the east lay Carriol and Pelli and Sangur and Kubal, and what had once been Urobb. Farr was an island now, cut away from the land.

In the mountains the fissure had snaked through the caves of Owdneet, already shattered by the earlier quakes. The magnificent grotto where Ramad had met the dark Seer was no more. All the early history of Ere, wrought in paintings on the stone ceiling and laid out in parchment scrolls, was gone, drowned in molten stone. The fissure's tail went north to end at last at the foot of Tala-charen. Tala-charen itself lay untouched.

Ere was split in two. "And the records of Ere's history are gone," Lobon said with remorse. He had not known that such a thing would so effect him. As if a record of himself, his memory of his own life, had been destroyed.

"We will write a new history then," Meatha said. "Tra-Hoppa will write it."

He looked at Jaspen. What would happen to the white-haired ones? Did they know who they were now? They had never known before, never known about Cadach, or even about one another. He knew from Meatha that Anchorstar and Merren Hoppa had no idea that they were sister and brother.

"We know now," Jaspen said. "We are the children of Cadach. Anchorstar knows, and Merren. Gredillon, in her own time knows. Our brother Thebon who moves through the unknown lands knows. Cadach has died now," she said, "and has been released, and so we are released—though that won't change what we are, and what we care about."

"And what was Cadach's crime?" Lobon said, not knowing if she would answer.

Skeelie spoke for her. "Cadach, in a time two years gone from this present time, showed the Kubalese how to use the drug MadogWerg—not to ease pain, but to control the minds of the Children of Ynell." She looked across at Meatha and saw that Meatha had gone pale. "Cadach by so doing," she said gently, "nearly took the life of his own son, of Anchorstar. Cadach, when he died, then was trapped in the tree."

"We knew not until now who our father was," Jaspen said, "or that we were atoning for him. I knew only that I guarded the stone. And that I waited."

"But how did you get the stone?" Meatha said. "How. . . ."

"I was an orphan child," Jaspen told them. "In Moramia. The slave of a miner. Another child, a slave, was treated cruelly—we all were, but he died from his beatings. It was he who kept the stone secret and hidden. He, Sechen, had been there on Tala-charen." She looked up at Skeelie. "You were there. You were on Tala-charen beside Ramad."

Skeelie nodded, a bond of sympathy and pain between them.

"When Sechen died, I took the stone, and a power came around me, a sense of—" she stared at them with her golden eyes and could not put to words the sense of the wonder, could only show them. They were caught in the vision of the

Luff' Eresi surrounding the child, speaking to the child. "They told me," Jaspen said, "that if I would return to the source of the stone, then the dark could never touch it. They said that it was very rare for them to guide the way of a mortal. They showed me where the dome was. And then they were gone, and I was alone in the slave hut with the stone to hide until I could escape.

"The wolves came to me in the night. I was terrified. But they spoke to me, and were so—I put my arms around them and I cried; for no one, except Sechen, had ever loved me.

"I followed them. They led me to the crystal dome, and then they went away. I—" She looked around, forgetting that the wolves had left them. "I missed them when they were gone. But . . . ." And she looked up now with a new brightness, a wonder they had not before seen. "But my sisters and my brothers will come now. We can be together if we wish." She took Skeelie's hand. "If you would wait with me, you could know—the woman who reared Ramad."

"I almost, once—I almost . . . ." Skeelie found to her consternation, that she was crying. She turned away and went to stand staring out through the clear dome.

All of Time that she had moved through, all the generations, all her life and Ram's seemed to culminate here. She was terrified and lost and exhilarated. She turned at last to Lobon and Meatha. "The Kubalese are driven back and docile," she said with certainty. "Kearb-Mattus crawls away beaten—alive, but injured and beaten." She sighed. "Carriol will rebuild now that which war and the violence of the land has destroyed. All Ere will begin anew now, as it has begun before. You—you will be a part of that building."

Lobon's voice caught. "And you, Mamen? You . . ."

But already she had turned toward the crystal door. She stood with it flung back as a big dark stallion winged down out of the sky and a man, broad of shoulder and bearded, leaped down and took her into his arms.

Chapter Ten

She was crying still, though her shoulders were straight where she was held tight against Canoldir. At last she turned away from him and took Lobon in a strong embrace, and then Meatha. She kissed the child Jaspen. "I will return to see Gredillon," she said. "If—if I can." Then she called to the mare who had been waiting close beside the dome, a bright russet mare. She mounted, was winging up through clouds beside Canoldir—whether to that place outside of Time or to another destination, none of them could tell.

Their own band of winged ones had drawn together, close to the crystal door. Meatha slid onto the back of the white mare, and Lobon chose Michennann. They were sky-borne, turned to wave down at the little pale figure beside the crystal dome. Then they looked ahead; and soon they saw below them, leaping across dunes like swift shadows, the two wolves heading south. *Will you come with us? Lobon asked them. We can carry you.* And the winged ones wheeled to await their answer.

But the wolves did not pause. *We will take our own way, Lobon of wolves,* Feldyn told him. *There is time now for us to travel in our own way. And time for you, Lobon, to ride a gentler wind.*

Time, now, for a kinder life, guarded by the power of the stones.

T H E   E N D

F   Murphy, Shirley
Rousseau

The joining of the
stone

DATE			
OC 1 5 '82	SEP 2 7 2016		
OC 2 7 '82			
NO 1 0 '82			
DE 1 3 82			
JAN 9			
JAN 20 1989			
SEP 1			
SEP 3 0 2009